PRAISE FOR ELINOR LIPMAN AND HER DELIGHTFUL SHORT STORY COLLECTION

INTO LOVE AND OUT AGAIN

"These stories are smart and funny and terrifically appealing."

—Marian Thurm, author of *Walking Distance*

"Lipman has a remarkable ear for the way certain women talk. . . . Her voice is natural and spontaneous and her observations have the authenticity of everyday life. . . ."

—Diane White, *The Boston Globe*

"*INTO LOVE AND OUT AGAIN* is an afternoon delight. Breezy, wry with just a shade of sex . . . a warm, playful curl-up-and-read volume that's over all too soon."

—*Ft. Worth Star Telegram*

"These zesty stories are comedies of manner in miniature, informed by Elinor Lipman's assured sense of the contemporary. Her witty observations of American ways of being in the 1980s would make Noël Coward proud."

—David Leavitt, author of *The Lost Language of Cranes* and *Family Dancing*

"If Jane Austen had been born about two centuries later, gone to Smith, then palled around with Fran Lebowitz, chances are she'd have written like Elinor Lipman. She is one of the last urbane romantics. . . ."

—Julia Glass, *Chicago Tribune*

Also by Elinor Lipman

Isabel's Bed
The Way Men Act
Then She Found Me

INTO LOVE AND OUT AGAIN

STORIES

ELINOR LIPMAN

WSP

WASHINGTON SQUARE PRESS
PUBLISHED BY POCKET BOOKS

New York London Toronto Sydney Tokyo Singapore

"Frankie's Soup" first appeared in *Cosmopolitan;* "Thick and Thin" in *Ascent;* "After Emily" in *Ladies' Home Journal;* "Catering" and "You're Right, I Know You're Right" in *Yankee.*

Grateful acknowledgment is made for permission to reprint the following copyrighted material:

"Theory" from *The Portable Dorothy Parker* by Dorothy Parker. Copyright 1928 by Dorothy Parker, renewed © 1956 by Dorothy Parker. Reprinted by permission of Viking Penguin Inc.

Excerpt from "A White Sport Coat and a Pink Carnation" by Marty Robbins. By permission of Mariposa Music, Inc.

Excerpt from "Some Enchanted Evening" by Richard Rodgers and Oscar Hammerstein II. Copyright © 1949 by Richard Rodgers and Oscar Hammerstein II. Copyright renewed, Williamson Music Co., owner of publication and allied rights throughout the Western Hemisphere and Japan. International copyright secured. All rights reserved. Used by permission.

WSP

A Washington Square Press Publication of
POCKET BOOKS, a division of Simon & Schuster Inc.
1230 Avenue of the Americas, New York, NY 10020

Published by arrangement with Viking Penguin Inc.
Library of Congress Catalog Card Number: 84-40319

ISBN: 0-671-65676-7

First Washington Square Press trade paperback printing November 1988

10 9 8 7 6 5 4 3

Cover design by Royce Becker

Printed in the U.S.A.

For my parents,
Julia Mazur Lipman and
Louis Saul Lipman

Theory

Into love and out again,
  Thus I went, and thus I go.
Spare your voice, and hold your pen—
  Well and bitterly I know
All the songs were ever sung,
  All the words were ever said;
Could it be, when I was young,
  Some one dropped me on my head?

—*Dorothy Parker*

People who made it possible,
for one reason or another:
Robert Austin, Arthur Edelstein,
Lizzie Grossman,
Mameve Medwed, Deborah Navas,
and Stacy Schiff

CONTENTS

INTO
LOVE
AND
OUT
AGAIN

Frankie's Soup

The Dunmores prepared their friends and relatives for Peter's engagement to me by announcing he was marrying into a bohemian family. I knew this was code, Darien-Connecticut code for "our son's marrying a Jewish girl." They are polite people, the Dunmores: they say the right thing and try hard to make me feel accepted, so I dismiss their quaint non sequiturs about loving bagels and the movie *Exodus* as the sincere efforts of sheltered WASPs. I love Peter, after all, and the way he doesn't notice suffixes on names, any more than he notices how his parents drop "Leibowitzes" and "Kaplans" and "Weinrebs"—casual acquaintances all—into conversations about The Club.

My mother isn't bohemian, even by Darien standards; just an old socialist who drifted to the right into left-wing activism.

She still lives in the seedy two-family house in Cambridge where I grew up, and is on every phone tree in every movement. In the early 1970s, when my father died, Louise went back to using her maiden name. She sent out printed announcements, stamped with a union bug, stating that the change did not impugn the memory of her husband. My father, Julian, had a master's degree in labor relations from Cornell and was a cabinetmaker.

My fiancé loves my mother in the way a wise parent loves a rebellious child. He thinks she is a charming case of arrested development, still in a stage of political indignation he experienced for a few weeks in 1970. When we are invited to her potluck fund-raisers, Peter dresses in his oldest corduroys and a black turtleneck and chuckles to himself in front of the mirror.

Louise likes Peter now and thinks it's hilarious I fell in love with a doctor. "Where did we go wrong?" she likes to ask with a twinkle in her dark brown eyes. Her friends have sons and daughters in the professions, but they are public defenders and inner-city pediatricians. I am somewhere in between: a sociology instructor at an expensive junior college.

But this is not about my mother, or the Dunmores, or even my wedding plans, except for a related complication. It's about Frankie, our friend, who moved two thousand miles away to Austin, Texas.

Frankie and Peter worked together while Peter and I lived together in a waterfront condominium paid for by his trust fund. We thought of Frankie as a lonely Chinese bachelor who needed mothering: his own parents, who called him by his given name, Foon Kee, spoke only of arranged marriages and unpaid debts when he dutifully called home.

Frankie was my escort and my pal. Together we saw the foreign films Peter didn't want to see and ordered the spiciest whole fish that Chinatown offered. We were brother and sister; brother and brother. Peter felt magnanimous and safe turning me over to Frankie for an evening out, and flattered: Dr. Frankie Hsu, elegant aesthete of two cultures, enjoyed my company enough to see one or both of us on his rare free nights. Peter even fantasized, I learned later, about presenting me to an undoubtedly horny Frankie who was too polite to seduce his occasional dates.

Frankie was attractive, all right, especially in his hospital whites which set off his shiny black hair and toast-colored skin. Patients adored him, too, for his gentle voice and unexpected jokes. His touch was so light that only the chill of his stethoscope woke up the dozing ones.

My mother was crazy about Frankie and asked him to all her functions. She dismissed his being a doctor as a first-generation lapse—getting the American dream out of the way so his children would be free to organize or to farm collectively. Louise flirted with him in her harmless, heavy-lidded way, all the while lobbying me in private for his suit.

"One word from you . . ." she would murmur in my ear as she passed the two of us dancing. I grimaced in annoyance, but gave it some thought those times when his cheek rested on my hair and I breathed in the smell of his sandalwood shaving soap and starched shirts. When the music ended and Frankie paused for just seconds before moving away, I imagined giving his hand a meaningful squeeze. Then I'd see Peter, such a known quantity, trustfully munching raw vegetables by the buffet table, and I'd resist the urge.

Louise's questions didn't help. "Does Peter like sex?" she asked me once in a voice so matter-of-fact that she could have been inquiring about the make of his car.

"Of course," I said.

"That's good," Louise said.

"Why would you ask me that?"

"I don't know," she said airily. "Just a thought." She often initiated mother-daughter talks like those, having reared me on frank discussions and anatomically correct names. She likes to discuss men and sex in a bold, offhand way so I will think she had affairs with many young socialists while an undergraduate at Barnard.

"So what do you two *talk* about?" she has asked in her chummy fashion. Or, "Is Peter's family very physical?"

She encouraged me to bring Frankie along to her parties when Peter was on call, and never acted as if one-third of our group was missing. She'd steer Frankie through the crowd, introducing him to people he'd met repeatedly; "Foon Kee!" Louise would call from corners of the room—never "Frankie"—as if to underscore the naturalized-American side of him that they all rooted for.

Peter grew lazy about taking me places and I grew careless. If he shrugged an ambivalent shrug over the play I wanted to see, I'd call Frankie up and make a date.

"Dinner first?" Frankie would ask.

"Dinner?" I'd ask Peter. He'd shrug again.

"Sure," I'd say. Then one night Frankie paused and added, "My place?"

"Okay," I answered slowly.

Frankie lived in a few rooms that were once servants' quarters in a Back Bay townhouse. They were tall and narrow; all white except for a shallow black marble fireplace and, on the night I was there, some flowers. He had placed single irises in pale green Perrier bottles, one on the mantel and one on the table; white linen napkins that looked starched and ironed stood on each white plate. The meal was Chinese, except for the champagne, and the best course, the pink soup, almost made me cry. It was a clear pale magenta, actually, and I found myself gazing into Frankie's eyes for longer than a mere platonic interval when he told me how he had made it: chicken for the stock; red pepper, red cabbage, red onion, one tomato. He strained it twice and garnished our bowls with pea pods and white mushrooms. I tasted it and sighed.

"How did you get it sweet?" I asked.

Frankie tipped his chair back and opened his tiny refrigerator. "I don't know what it's called in English," he said, moving bottles from shelf to shelf. When he brought forth the secret of his amazing soup—a dried California fig—I wanted to kiss the hand that offered it.

Shrimp came next, and beef with bitter melon. Dessert was whole strawberries, hulls and all, piled into clear glass teacups. Frankie left me at the table and made coffee at the stove. I felt so sad for the few minutes I was alone in his stark white living room; sad that a man who stuck irises in pale green bottles and strawberries in clear teacups, apologizing in both instances for not having the proper vessels, was alone. Frankie brought the ceramic coffeepot to the table and I smiled up at him. He poured each of us a cup, frowning, then pulled me slowly to my feet and took my face in his two warm hands.

"Are we going to kiss?" I asked.

"If you want to," he answered.

It was like Frankie himself: sweet and intense. We had kissed before, plenty of times, even on the lips; hello and good-bye usually, and sometimes pecks for solace or congratulations. But not like this. Peter and I hadn't even kissed like this, intertwined, coffee getting cold, pulses throbbing. This could change everything, I thought. Frankie and I are not going to end up naked on his convertible sofa and then go back to being friends.

And Peter. He'd find someone else before long, a Protestant this time; a blue-eyed blonde. They would live a quiet, secure life—the one I had planned, *my* quiet secure life with in-laws who spoke English, silver service for twenty-four, and a robust husband who wouldn't leave me widowed like Louise. I moved away from Frankie and picked up my coffee cup.

I was sure this was only physical and it would pass. Frankie was one of the boys you kissed at fifteen, hormones coursing; one in a series of handsome ethnic boys I felt passionately about in high school, at the same time knowing we'd part at graduation and marry other people. I didn't look back at them very wistfully. I would get over Frankie, too.

"Peter and I . . ." I began, not sure of what would follow.

"I'll talk to Peter."

"Don't," I said automatically.

"Marry me," he said softly. I shut my eyes to block the images of Frankie's pink soup and the choreography of our kiss. I thought about Chinese-American children we would have with bangs hanging straight to their eyebrows; Jewish-Chinese-American babies with my pink Polish cheeks and his prize-winning cheekbones. But there was no canopied crib in my vision, no English perambulator, no live-in help except for the crowd of needy Chinese cousins. The little Eurasian faces blurred into Peter's sturdy Yankee features. "I can't," I said. Frankie stared at me for a long time.

"Swear to me that you love him," he said finally. "More than this."

"It's different," I explained. Peter was so uncomplicated, so all-American and accepted, that I could look down the road and see the terrain of a whole life with him. There would be few surprises, few peaks and fewer valleys. Louise would roll her eyes with boredom and start political arguments at our dinner parties, but at least they would be catered. I would be Mrs. Dunmore and I would teach one or two courses a semester and not worry about getting tenure.

My evening with Frankie came into focus and I felt on the verge of saying something quite mature to explain what happened: that some beauty created by Frankie, some fairy dust he sprinkled on my food in his tiny kitchen alcove made me forget my plans. I wanted to go home to Peter's mahogany bed with the carved headboard—a Dunmore family heirloom—and put my dinner in perspective. By the time I had my coat on, my guilt had receded. It had just been a matter of timing, I thought, with the kiss coming after a meal whose wine and beauty caught me off guard. I did love Peter, I assured myself. I did.

"Good night," I said brightly at his door. "And thank you for a delicious dinner." With his fingertips pressed together, Frankie bowed a quick servile nod and said something in Chinese I didn't understand.

The phone rang as soon as I got home: Peter's good-night call from the hospital. "How was it?" he asked.

"Fun," I said. Frankie kissed me and I almost slept with him and now he wants to marry me, I thought.

"I'm waiting for a head scan," Peter said. "The machine's down. I'm reading *People* magazine."

"Lucky you," I said.

"How come you're back so early?" he asked.

"I came straight home after dinner."

"Why?"

"It's a long story."

"I'm coming home," Peter said.

When he got there I told him the truth: about the meal; the way purple onion and red cabbage tint chicken broth and how Frankie had made up the recipe himself. Peter listened patiently and looked sad.

"I wouldn't kiss someone else," he said when I had finished. Then: "Poor Frankie."

I pointed out, in what he considers to be my litigious Jewish way, that I chose him over Frankie despite our lack of a formal engagement; he apologized, in what I consider to be his obsequious Protestant way, for implying that I was unfaithful. He went back to the hospital and I went to bed after we kissed quite tenderly and discussed taking Grandmother Dunmore's one-and-a-half-carat round diamond from the vault, finally.

I called Frankie and described what had happened to us at his apartment. "When two people are fond of each other, and one is male and the other is female, and they're heterosexual, it's natural for them to think about sex under certain favorable conditions."

Frankie was silent.

"Besides," I added cheerfully, "your parents would disown you."

" 'Find a nice Chinese girl,' in other words?"

"Don't be mad at me," I said.

I discussed the evening with Louise months afterward. It wasn't a confession or even a mother-daughter heart-to-heart, but an answer to a casual question.

"What's new with Foon Kee?" she asked me.

"I don't know."

"Is he away?"

"Sort of." I gave her an abbreviated account of dinner and dessert at Frankie's place, and she sighed. "He's so attractive—those marvelous bones and those gorgeous hands. I bet he's fantastic in bed."

"I didn't stay," I told her.

"Pity."

"I wouldn't cheat on Peter."

"Salt of the earth that he is," she muttered. I asked her why she hated Peter, and she looked surprised.

"I don't hate him at all. I just don't think you love him."

She wanted to hear me say that I was marrying for money and stability and that I was spurning Frankie for his Third-Worldness and tuition debts. "I love him," I said.

"Peter?"

"Peter," I hissed.

Louise sighed. "It's our fault—your father's and mine. We should have moved to the suburbs . . . bought a little place with a yard and a station wagon so you'd have roots. And security. Worked real jobs. Let you have white bedroom furniture—the kind with gold trim."

"French provincial."

"French provincial. Then you wouldn't need to marry a Republican." She shook her head sadly. "Poor Foon Kee. He's nuts over you."

"Forget it," I said.

Louise's voice tightened. "One of you finally gets up the nerve to acknowledge what's going on, and you run home to Peter—he of the white skin and *Mayflower* credentials." She took my chin in her hand and spoke softly. "I've seen the way you and Frankie dance together."

I jerked my head away. "Don't do this to me," I said. Louise picked up my left hand and frowned at the Dunmore diamond, enormous in its new Tiffany setting.

"You know what you want," she said. "You always have."

Mrs. Dunmore insisted on shopping with Louise for their wedding outfits. We had all decided to let her plan the ceremony and reception. She was relieved to be running the show and willing to commute any distance for a consultation. Even Peter, as kind and unironic as he is, saw that his mother was worried Louise would wear black leotards or the equivalent in bohemian formal attire. She wanted champagne and finger sandwiches and white cake, and feared my relatives expected "ethnic food."

So it was at a Saturday lunch at Lord & Taylor that Mrs. Dunmore, while talking about cutaways and morning jackets, asked if that nice Chinese boy, the doctor, was going to be an usher.

"Afraid not," Louise said. And in her breezy liberal style told my future mother-in-law that Frankie and I had had a liaison.

"Oh, something like that," she reconstructed later, her eyes wide with surprise at my distress. "I didn't go into detail."

"There wasn't any detail to go into," I said.

Louise dismissed my anger with a superior smile. "Believe me, Sweetie, all she's thinking about is color schemes. I know her type. She didn't even hear me."

I learned later that Mrs. Dunmore had gone straight home to Connecticut and her bed. She refused to say at first that it was more than just the strain of shopping and diplomacy. But in the middle of the night she rang for sherry and called Mr. Dunmore to her side.

"There's something you must know," she had said, beginning a tearful monologue which lasted until sunup. The gist of it was that Peter was marrying into a family of hippie Bolsheviks who believed in free love and thought money was a dirty word. Worst of all, even though I *appeared* to have fallen far from the tree, dressing well and teaching at that nice school, I had been unfaithful to the dearest boy in the world.

Mr. Dunmore had jumped into his Peugeot and driven two hours to have breakfast at the hospital with his betrayed son. The story I had told Peter months before—dinner and a kiss—returned to him full-blown: Frankie and I were lovers, according to Mr. Dunmore, and lovers of the worst kind; lying, secret, minority lovers who had betrayed a best friend and fiancé.

Peter didn't know where to begin setting him straight. He vowed that I had revealed every detail of my innocent dinner with Frankie the minute I came home, unbetrothed and unobligated as I had been. Practically in tears, Peter called me at school and said, "Here. Tell my father what happened at Frankie's flat."

In the end it was easiest to blame Louise, who didn't mind one bit anyway. In public, she apologized to the Dunmores for her carelessness; in private, in her blithe exasperating way, she blamed Mrs. Dunmore for taking such a bourgeois view of something so beautiful.

I scolded Louise several times before the wedding, and phoned whenever I remembered a family indiscretion she might mention in a toast. If she asked me a question that was slightly personal, or talked about Frankie, I pursed my lips and ignored her.

Frankie was invited to our wedding in June—proof of our harmless platonic feelings—and he came. His date was stunning, a blonde oncologist Peter recognized from the hospital.

Louise, in a dress one shade paler than hot pink, walked me down the aisle. She nodded triumphantly to familiar faces, pleased with her token assault on tradition. Peter, dear and smiling among the pots of white camellias, waited at the altar.

Close to the end of our walk, we passed Foon Kee. Louise, ever dramatic, paused for a moment; I left her there as if our separation was rehearsed.

After the ceremony, I watched my new mother-in-law greet Frankie with a tight smile as he passed through the receiving line. Mr. Dunmore shook hands manfully. Louise, naturally, hugged Foon Kee as if he needed comfort. He glided past Peter and me, his eyes fixed on some other faces; he didn't speak, but kissed us both good-bye.

Thick and Thin

My therapist and my mother say I exaggerate my size and lack perspective on my body image. "You don't see me naked," I tell them. Neither does anyone else. I've been fat for three years now and without a man for just as long. Other fat women I know have pictures of skinny models taped to their refrigerators, and size-eight dresses challenging them from their closets. And while my libido reminds me that my former body had sex on a somewhat regular basis, I'm having trouble getting motivated.

The only men who flirt with me are the husbands of my friends. They say sexual things to me, always in front of their wives: "what-a-lot-of-woman" remarks which are supposed to make me feel dangerous but only point out the inadequacies of my caftans and ponchos. All it shows me is that they read adult magazines and know the fat-girl fantasies—our pillow-breasted bodies, our foam-rubber buttocks, our private white skin. In truth, they flirt because I'm safe, and I'm safe because I'm fat. Anyone can see they're married to gaunt women.

I've been fat since I finished college and began eating seriously. I had never had my own apartment, my own refrigerator, my own freezer; never been at the helm of my own shopping cart; never had so much time to myself. *I* see my size as an environmental problem—too much Sara Lee beckoning me from the dairy case. Dr. Katz would like to make it an issue of self-worth. He is subtle, but I know the theories: I am fat because I am denying my sexuality; I'm afraid of intimacy; I fear that if I were thin I'd be rejected for something more intrinsic than adipose tissue. "I'm fat because I eat," I tell Dr. Katz. He chips away at me weekly and my mother pays the bills.

Actually, I'm looking for intimacy. I have had three lovers: two when I was average-sized and one when I was crossing over to heavy. I'm satisfied with three, historically. It sounds varied, even successful, but not enough to cause problems with Dr. Katz, who would see neurosis in large numbers. He implies, along with my mother and thin friends, that I will not find a boyfriend as long as I stay fat. I tell them I don't want another Barry—the third and last one—who can't see past my dress size; who loves me as long as I weigh less than he. My fourth lover will not read ideal-weight charts to me from milk cartons, or care that my bathing suits all have skirts. He will think my body is beautiful and desirable, and whisper my name huskily after we make love.

I have unrealistic expectations, Dr. Katz says. I'm judging people by a fairy tale test, casting myself as the Beast and holding out for Beauty. "Do you like fat men?" he asks. "Is someone a bad person if they prefer their lovers thin?"

"Yes," I say.

Dr. Katz believes my sarcasm is a problem. If *I* call myself a fatty, a chubbo, a blimp, Miss Piggy, or tons of fun before someone else sizes me up as a little overweight (his description), I turn my body into a parody that no one has to take seriously. Not true, I argue. Just once—and I'm sorry I ever told him—I introduced myself to an unattached male, who was blatantly avoiding me at a dinner party, as Martha Rooney, Fat Spinster. The guy, whose name was Keith something, just blinked and excused himself coldly, and left before dessert. I didn't tell Katz that I ate Keith's portion of the walnut torte.

It was a Saturday night in June when I met Carl Grebber in line at the Orson Welles Cinema. "Martha Rooney?" a man's voice asked. I turned around, hopeful, but didn't see a familiar face. "Martha?" said the handsomest of the men I had seen in Harvard Square that night. "Carl Grebber," he offered quietly, knowing the exclamations of astonishment his name would provoke.

I gasped. Carl Grebber had been the college fat man, a hugely obese classmate who dressed in gigantic denim overalls and made noises when he breathed. Everyone knew Carl, his name, and his eating habits: cafeteria workers gave him seconds and thirds on his first trip through the line, and it was rumored he paid a surcharge on his board. He had been extremely smart and funny, specializing in fat-man jokes at his own expense. No one had felt sorry for Carl because he was happy and popular and so clearly to blame for his own enormousness. Impossible to view as a sex object, Carl was befriended by lots of women, including me. He was so comfortable, so easy to talk to, so safe.

I had thought of Carl Grebber often since I graduated and got fat. I have even heard echoes of Carl's humor when I call myself names and eat heartily in public. I searched this thin man's face for hints of Carl Grebber. "It's me," he said. "I've been dieting."

"I'm sorry," I said, thrown off by the distinct jaw and visible cheekbones. "I can't see you in there."

"It's me. Former sideshow, Carl Grebber." The self-deprecation sounded authentic. I put out my hand. "Kind of spooky," I said.

"Try it from this side," he answered.

He told me he had lost one hundred and eighty pounds over twenty-six months, part of it in a hospital, fasting. I assumed he was ecstatic with his new body, his new *beauty* I thought to myself, and said so.

He shrugged. "It's hard. Real hard."

"I know. Dieting is the worst."

He said he was used to that part. "It's the other stuff. My self-image." This favorite subject of Dr. Katz's caused a flutter in my stomach. The line had started to move forward and I was afraid the movie would break us up. I asked Carl if he would like to go someplace and talk instead. He suggested coffee at his place.

On the way to the Square, he seemed to be concentrating on his stride, taking long, bobbing steps, the studied walk of a gangly teenager. The obese Carl had walked with an open stance and a sway to push his massive thighs back and forth. "I can't get over this," I repeated every few blocks. "Carl *Grebber*." After a few minutes of silence, he stopped and spoke. "I tend to think that the people who are most flabbergasted found me the most grotesque."

I protested, citing my own fat as proof of my empathy.

"Don't compare yourself to me," he said.

I wanted to say the right thing—that he always had a handsome face and hadn't been grotesque, but it wasn't true. Girls in my dorm, and I along with them, had made Carl Grebber jokes throughout our four years. The slightest suggestion of a naked Carl Grebber—we imagined an amorphous, pink, hairless, sexless body—never failed to evoke squeals of disgust. Even now, as we walked, I could not think some sexual thought about his beautifully bony hands or prominent clavicle without having an image of his former knockwurstian fingers and doughy neck shoot across my brain. I squeezed his hand, secretly marveling at the feel of it, and tried to match his sad grimace.

Carl had a narrow bed in his studio apartment, a marriage of his new body with his old sex life. It was a safe man's room, with no props for seduction. Like Carl himself, the furnishings were spare and trim, even stylish, with touches of Cambridge understatement.

He kissed me without advance notice while we waited for coffee to drip. It was a tentative kiss, a question, accomplished with only our lips touching. Maybe Carl just kisses, I thought.

Sweet little inexperienced kisses. Maybe we would kiss on his butcherblock loveseat, then walk back to the Orson Welles Cinema and hold hands during the movie. We would be girlfriend and boyfriend in an Old World way, and one day he would touch my breasts while we made out.

Carl touched my breasts that moment, as soon as I returned his kiss. He made a noise which I interpreted to be a moan of pleasure. I let him continue touching me through my clothes, too startled either to stop him or to respond.

"Martha?" he whispered.

I guess I put my arms around him. He felt thin, but wonderful. I touched the back of his neck and felt the buttons of his vertebrae. The curly hair that had once been the finishing touch to his look of clownish excess was short and crisp now. What a beautiful man he was.

My long dress of cotton gauze didn't allow for any undressing in stages. When the time seemed right, I lifted my arms over my head so Carl could slip it off, and revealed my body in underpants alone. He actually gasped and pulled me against him, holding tight to my upper arms. He was so clearly moved by the thighs and waist and breasts I had come to hate that I walked to the narrow bed first.

There wasn't room to lie side by side, so Carl lowered his light body on mine. We stayed that way, his cheek resting on my chest. "I just want to hold you," he repeated whenever I moved my hips under his. After about an hour, Carl got up and put on his clothes. "Coffee?" was all he said. I didn't ask if we were finished, or say I was hoping for intercourse. He looked more cheerful, even sated. I supposed our relationship would escalate and we'd be bona fide lovers soon.

Carl drank his coffee with his hand on my thigh, squeezing at regular intervals. His touch became methodical, inching toward my knee with each squeeze. He was absorbed, curious, admiring, and I saw in his face that his fondling had nothing to do with my pleasure. He wanted my fat.

"What are you doing?" I murmured, laying my hand on his to stop the exploration. He squeezed its plumpness too.

"Do you mind?" he asked, looking into my eyes for the first time, grabbing my thigh with more resolve. I rose and dressed quickly. Over my shoulder I saw him consider his own thighs and knead them, stopping after a few disappointing squeezes. "It's been so long," he said.

I couldn't eat much that weekend, and lost four pounds by my next session with Dr. Katz. The following week, he noticed a change. I didn't tell him about my evening with Carl, but made up a story to cover my sudden motivation: that I was asked to be a bridesmaid at a summer wedding and wanted to look presentable in my off-the-shoulder chiffon print. Katz accepted the story eagerly, as I knew he would, especially when I invented a longing for a certain usher.

I couldn't tell him what happened, that I had lost my appetite; that the sight and feel of my thighs spreading over my kitchen chairs sickened me; that I ate standing up when I ate at all. But when I lost the excess that Carl wanted, and I still felt bad, I knew it was time to talk.

Katz couldn't hear enough about Carl. Awed by his weight loss, and swooning with anticipation over self-image problems, Katz took Carl's side. One hundred and eighty pounds, he repeated reverently. Imagine his turmoil.

"He used me," I said.

Katz disagreed. Carl must be inexperienced. Perhaps I didn't realize his fondling was foreplay.

"What about *my* feelings?" I said to remind him my mother was paying for Martha Rooney's mental health, not Carl Grebber's.

"What *about* your feelings?" he threw back.

We role-played a telephone call to Carl.

Me: Hello, Carl?

Katz: Martha!

"He's not going to recognize my voice. Let's do it over," I said.

Me: Carl? (hold up hand to silence Katz) This is Martha . . . Rooney.

Katz: Martha!

"No. He's angry. He hates me for rejecting him. Let me talk until I give you a signal."

Me: Carl? Martha Rooney. I've been feeling badly about running out of your apartment after we . . . (to Katz) I don't know what to call it.

Katz: After we *made love*. It's different things to different people, Martha.

This went on for weeks. When I finally called Carl on a Sunday night months later, he sounded happy to hear from me. We talked briefly and made a date for lunch.

Carl was already seated when I arrived at the sandwich shop in Harvard Square the next day. I hadn't told him I was thinner, and I saw he was fat again—not obese like before, but rounder and thicker everywhere. He was no longer beautiful, with the edges and angles blurred by his new flesh, but he looked less fragile and guarded this way, and I felt relieved. I waved. He smiled and pulled out the other chair. "Have you ordered?" I asked.

He picked up the menu and studied it. "I'll have a burger. With everything."

"Black coffee for me," I told the waitress.

"When did you go on a diet?" he asked when we were alone.

"Right after I saw you."

"Because of what happened at my place?"

I shrugged. "I wasn't trying. I haven't felt like eating."

"I'm just the opposite—when I'm upset, I eat." He pinched several inches of his own cheek. "I've been upset."

I touched his face where his fingers had left white dents in the ruddy flesh. It was as soft as old flannel. Carl covered my hand with his.

The waitress brought our meal. Carl discarded the top half of his roll and blotted the hamburger between two paper napkins. I sipped my coffee and we talked. It was as if we were back in school, lingering over a meal and skipping class. Nobody would have paired us up then, or ever taken us for more than friends. But at the restaurant, we were a couple, staying past the luncheon crowd, talking intently, and me eating French fries from Carl's plate without asking—the way people do when they are very close.

After Emily

Everyone in the department wanted babies after Susan Rosenzweig had Emily at thirty-eight and did it all so well. She breast-fed discreetly at faculty meetings and brought Emily to class in a calico-lined wicker basket. She hadn't been tired or nauseated, and had looked wonderful, too—thin all over with just the bump. Amniocentesis confirmed that her baby girl had the right number of chromosomes; ultrasonography gave her a Polaroid picture of some barely identifible parts to frame.

Things were different for me when I had my babies years ago, far away from Boston. I am excluded from the new sorority of older primiparas because my daughters are in junior high school and my colleagues know I had anesthesia at both deliveries. I've never felt bad about it until now—about the spinals (nobody even knows about the forceps); about Paul waiting it out in the fathers' lounge; about not breast-feeding. They would pity me if they knew my first pregnancy wasn't planned, and the second a rush job eight months after Laura so I could get on with school, our family complete.

Some of the women do ask me about parenting, but fewer and fewer since word got out that I didn't keep a journal during either pregnancy. It is Susan they turn to for first-person accounts of labor and delivery, and for reassurances about the ecstasy of motherhood. And while they are kind to my daughters when they visit the college, their greatest compliments and most foolish, uninhibited behavior are reserved for tiny Emily.

Monica Shaw, an adjunct faculty member who is just thirty-one, came in this week and said she had had the same dream twice: she was dressed for a dinner party in a peacock-blue silk dress when a wet spot appeared at each breast. The leaking-milk dreams, as she calls them, have left her shaken, and she has been obsessing about babies ever since. She thinks it may be a signal from her body that her fertility is declining and that she had better conceive before it is too late. We sent her to Peter Offenbach in the Psych Department, who did his thesis on the dreams of single women.

I've been dreaming about babies, too. There's a lot of laughter in these dreams—mine, Paul's, our daughters'—in which tiny darling infants on the half shell are brought to our tables by waiters. My co-workers interpret them to mean, quite literally, that I want more children, but I don't think that's it. I'd just like to have my babies now in the Eighties, with a coach, and do it right.

After Emily

My children are following the events in my office with great interest. My older daughter finds it fascinating that my pregnant colleagues are at least as old as I am.

"Why didn't they have children before?" she asks.

"They weren't ready until now."

"Were you ready when Deb and I were born?"

"Of course," I say, lying.

I was twenty-four and married less than a year when I got pregnant with Laura. Paul and I were students, living off meager salaries as teaching assistants. I was even on the Pill. The month Laura was conceived, I missed a weekend's worth of my prescription while on a camping trip; just enough, apparently, to let me ovulate. New York State had the country's only legal abortions, and we considered making the ten-hour drive. "Is it an impossible situation?" the New York doctor asked me over the telephone. "Would you not be able to care for a child right now?"

It didn't occur to me that his questions were perfunctory. I thought he was seeking Truth and weeding out the merely inconvenienced. We stayed in Ohio and telephoned prospective grandparents. For weeks Paul paced in our one-bedroom apartment repeating softly to himself, "I'm ready . . . you know, I'm really ready . . ."

In our graduate-English circles, we were the only couple with a baby, and seventeen months later, the only one with two. We became houseparents in an undergraduate dorm in exchange for free room and board, and spent nights cursing the noise that came through the cinderblock walls or trying to muffle the crying within them.

I don't remember my daughters as infants very clearly, but I do have vivid custodial memories: washing the little plastic bags for reuse in Playtex Nursers; zipping two hungry, kicking toddlers into snowsuits for three trips a day to the dining hall. We ate our meals early, apologetically, at remote tables, grateful for any silly noise or approving smile from fellow diners.

The girls are twelve and thirteen now, and their father and I have been divorced four years. People mix them up, forget who is older, which one plays the flute and which one takes gymnastics. "We should've had twins," Paul once grumbled after his weekend with the girls. "At least we'd get some mileage out of it."

"We should have waited," I answer when they aren't around to hear me. And I think of my colleague Winnie Babcock, thirty-nine, pregnant with her second after a thirteen-year hiatus. "Like having a first child all over again," she marvels, except for the changes: midwives, disposable diapers, no talcum powder, Dr. Spock's new nonsexist pronouns and, of course, breasts instead of bottles. She's due in six weeks and we had a coed shower for her in the English Department conference room. Christopher got several carved wooden pull toys, hand-stitched quilts, and an anatomically correct doll. Winnie and her husband did some of their breathing techniques for us. They are looking forward to Christopher's birth and to managing the pain together.

"Do you want another?" the women ask from time to time, knowing how the baby boom affects me. "Not exactly," I answer. But I have been looking at baby pictures of the girls lately, forcing myself to remember how it felt to be tired all the time. What I feel instead is a craving to crawl inside the photos, kiss the fat cheeks, and bury my face in the ticklish bellies. I want my babies back.

Our older male colleagues shake their heads and tell us how their wives stayed in the hospital for ten days after childbirth, didn't take the babies out in winter, and sterilized everything. They also say they're glad they didn't have to watch.

"And why is that?" Susan Rosenzweig asks Roger Egan, father of four.

"You know," he says.

"I'm afraid you're going to have to spell it out for me," Susan says with a wink for the women present. Roger looks around for help. "I'm not asking too personal a question, am I?"

"Not really."

"Louis says that Emily's birth was the greatest moment of his life," she offers.

"Some men really like it," says Roger.

"But you don't think you would?"

Roger shakes his head. "If you're not used to that kind of thing it can affect you later."

"How?" Susan asks, widening her eyes in mock perplexity.

"You know . . . relations."

"Ohhh," she says with exaggerated comprehension. "You mean that seeing a baby come out of your wife's vagina puts you off? You lose your sexual appetite?"

Roger grimaces. Those of us listening and those who hear about it later enjoy this exchange immensely. Roger is not a sensitive fellow who deserves more delicacy, but the master of the unfunny off-color joke, particularly those composed at the expense of female students. His name comes up regularly at Women's Committee meetings.

Monica Shaw is thinking seriously about becoming a single parent, and the word is out around the college. She has received two obscene notes from would-be inseminators, a stern caution with religious overtones from, we think, the secretary in the Russian Department, and several obnoxious remarks from Roger.

"I know I don't have a Nobel Prize," he says, "but I am better looking than Gabriel García Márquez . . . and I could do the job the old-fashioned way."

"You're all talk, Egan," Susan says on Monica's behalf. "Besides, you've got enough kids for an assistant professor with no hope of advancement." She smiles just enough to make Roger think she's teasing.

We all look up to Susan, who teaches our Bible-as-Literature course and who enjoys a cult following. When she announced more than a year ago that she was pregnant, I sensed it was only a matter of time before more babies would be born to the English faculty. She hadn't told any of us that she and Louis were trying—actually taking her temperature and having intercourse by the calendar—so the announcement was stunning.

Monica and I feel a kinship since we're both single and outside the baby boom's inner circle. It took hold in the faculty lunchroom the day Polly Linnehan, thirty-five, announced she was expecting. Monica put her tray down next to mine and said she hoped I wouldn't ruin her lunch with another announcement of a maternal nature.

"Unlikely," I said.

"That's what Polly said."

"Surprised?"

"Nothing surprises me anymore: Susan, *Winnie* for God's sake—her husband's forty-six. Now Polly. A year ago she and Martin were looking at condos with spiral staircases and free-standing fireplaces. You can't tell me this was planned."

"It was. She had her IUD taken out after Emily was born." Monica pushed her chair closer to mine and lowered her voice. "Sometimes I think I want a baby more than anything. Other times I feel . . . not so sure. Peter thinks I'm confusing a baby with wanting a relationship."

"Peter?" I asked.

"You know—Offenbach. Psych Department. Either way, he says I've got time."

"He's right."

"I know. But how much fun is it going to be having a kid five years from now? Things might change. I might not be teaching here. And there might be a baby bust by then."

"I had mine during a baby bust," I told her. "You love them just as much."

"Of course you do," she said politely.

Paul has written to me and sent separate notes to the girls, announcing that my replacement is pregnant. We're all surprised: Paul's new wife brags about her indifference to babies and her lack of maternal instinct. She treats the girls casually and democratically, and gives them wine with their meals. Paul writes me that he is "thrilled and awed" by the pregnancy, adding indelicately that he is ready for parenting in a way he couldn't have been before. To the girls he says, "I'll always love you two in a special way, my pumpkin girls, my first- and second-born." No psychological mandate moves him to assure me that my pregnancies, our babies, his first marriage are what he'll cherish most. I sense that his new wife didn't read his notes to the girls, but had worked on mine with Paul. A postscript in her handwriting says she is feeling fine and hopes I can be happy for them.

I wonder if the depression I feel is jealousy. I distract myself by thinking of a gift—something appropriate for children of a first marriage to give a new half-sibling. I also wonder if I will add my name to the card I'll enclose. I hadn't let the girls attend their father's wedding in the college chapel on the campus where we taught and where the bride took our courses. Their absence hurt Paul (my intentions exactly) and prompted the bride to tell a department member who didn't boycott the wedding that I was a small person.

My daughters call me at work several times a day. Most of their calls are requests for mediation: Laura is pulling rank on Deborah who wasn't going to bother me except that my other *retarded* daughter won't let her make English muffin pizzas even though she's dying of starvation.

"Look," I say. "You may have an English muffin. You may not use the mozzarella. Laura needs it for the lasagna."

Susan, in the next cubicle, hears my end of the conversation. "My God," she breathes, "imagine coming home to a cooked dinner."

"Not every night," I say modestly.

"But still . . . they must do things like set the table, wash dishes, *talk* to you. And no fussy period between four and six."

I laugh. "You'd be surprised . . ."

"Let's see—Emily's four months old and yours are . . . ?"

"Laura's thirteen and Deb—"

"Twelve-plus years from now I'll be where you are, lasagna on the table."

I hear stirrings from Emily's basket, then the cry of hunger we have all come to recognize. "Emmy's up," Roger announces dryly from his corner.

Winnie Babcock's Christopher was born last week after eighteen hours of hard labor and three hours of pushing. He weighed nine pounds, two ounces, and he nurses vigorously. It was a bad time for Winnie, and she's not coming back this semester. I saw her at the hospital a few days after the birth and she was in a great deal of pain from an enormous episiotomy. "It wasn't this bad last time," she told me.

"They drugged us so we wouldn't remember."

"I must have been more elastic. All these young kids are

jogging back and forth to the nursery and peeing on their own. I feel like their grandmother." I kissed her and told her she had the most beautiful baby on the floor, and promised I'd visit her at home. Waiting at the elevator, I heard her call my name.

"One more thing," Winnie said when I returned to her bedside. She shifted on her hip bone and winced. "Don't tell Polly how terrible it was."

My ex-husband's wife is having a daughter, according to the amnio results, and my girls are pleased. They claim they prefer a baby half-sister to a brother, but I suspect they are waging a gender contest between me and their stepmother. I also think they know Paul will be less thrilled and awed by the same old pink stretchies than he'd be by the novelty of blue. Meanwhile, they report, the expectant mother is losing her hair in bunches and has acne. I send my regards every Friday.

"What did you do about day-care when your kids were small?" asks Susan. Emily has outgrown her wicker basket and wants to creep.

"Students," I tell her. "Especially the ones who wouldn't take money." Susan makes a face. I know she wants a mature woman; preferably a mother and nonsmoker; ideally, French-speaking. Emily, reclining at her usual sixty-degree angle in an infant seat, begins to fuss. "Let me," I say.

Susan sighs. She reaches down to her bottom drawer for a plastic pad, a disposable diaper, and a carton of pop-up wipes.

"Home away from home," I say.

"Not quite." She leans over and kisses Emily's nose. "Love this girl," she croons, "love this baby girl." Emily whimpers. "Let me dump this," says Susan, picking up the diaper and putting the baby in my arms. I walk around Susan's cubicle, bouncing Emily on my shoulder.

"Quite the touch," a voice says—Roger's. I ignore him and change directions. "Where's Mama?"

"She'll be right back."

"I think little one wants something you can't provide," he adds, his favorite euphemism for breast-feeding.

"She's tired," I snap.

"Where I come from, babies are put into cribs when they're tired. But I guess that's too old-fashioned for Professor Rosenzweig." It seems disloyal to Susan, and to Emily, to admit I agree with Roger. I pat Emily's back without conviction. She burps an adult burp and spits up on my shoulder. Roger snickers. I hand him the baby.

I expect to find Susan, as usual, trapped in conversation with a Bible-as-Literature devotee. Instead, she is standing inside one of the bathroom stalls. I ask if she's okay.

"What time is it?"

"Ten to three."

"Shit," she says softly and blows her nose.

"Are you ill?"

"I have a seminar at three and I'm not coping very well. . . . Is Emily with you?"

"Roger's got her."

Susan laughs a short cynical laugh. She opens the door and meets me at the sink. "It's hard," she says. "I don't want to be here."

"You're tired."

"Louis can't really get up with her in the middle of the night. . . ."

"She'll be sleeping through soon. They all do eventually."

"The books say eight weeks."

"Fuck the books." Susan smiles begrudgingly, and I put my arm around her shoulders. "Cancel your seminar. We'll go to my house and have the girls watch Emily while you nap." Susan nods and allows one sob to escape.

The girls and I dance and sing and make rude noises to amuse Emily while her mother sleeps. For a while, the three of us perform together; then we take turns. The baby bends at the waist and wails into her own lap whenever the antics stop.

"This is an incredible drag," my thirteen-year-old says when her shift ends. Her sister, the gymnast, performs a slow, perfect backwards arch to the floor and rises to a handstand. Baby Emily blinks hard. Our gymnast flails her legs in the air, and the baby smiles. Laura and I cheer.

"I can't keep this up indefinitely," says Deborah, her face rosy and getting redder. She springs to her feet. The baby flops forward and wails. Laughing, we dance and sing some more.

Catering

Lionel became interested in cooking the summer he took the Massachusetts Bar. Quiche was just catching on that year; people were eating their spinach and mushrooms raw, buying their coffee beans whole, saying "tofu." I gave him a gift subscription to *Bon Appétit* when he was hired by Hill, Metcalfe in Boston. Soon he was roaming the North End on his lunch hour in search of cracked veal bones. After two years with the firm, he left law and me.

This is his job now: Lionel shops and cooks dinner one night each week, Sunday through Thursday, for five different women. His meals are delicious, healthful, feminine: poached fish fillets and boned chicken, vegetables in vinaigrette sauce, soufflés, lots of fruit and cheese and chocolate; delicate, thoughtful meals that women love with their dry white wines. He wanted only five clients, five women with good taste. He says he found them.

There were no advertisements, no mass mailings. Lionel simply left his chocolate-brown announcements in a Newbury Street women's shop which sells man-tailored suits and expensive pocketbooks. The cream-colored calligraphy was the perfect touch:

CATERING TO YOU

Light Suppers and Conversation
for Gourmet Career Women

Lionel Berens, Esq.
References

They were so much like our wedding invitations, in color and size and succinctness, that I cried when I opened the familiar brown envelope and ignored several days' messages from Lionel on my answering machine.

He tells me more than I can bear about his clients—their preferences in food, their allergies, what they look like, and whether they have large breasts. They are all attracted to Lionel, who is tall and thin and looks very much like an off-duty attorney in his corduroy trousers and plaid wool shirts. His curly brown hair with its gray streaks, his rimless glasses, and the way he hums "I've Grown Accustomed to Her Face" when he minces garlic on a cutting board only add to his appeal.

He arrives at his customers' condominiums cheerful and confident at 5:45. The doormen and neighbors recognize him by his wicker basket and the wonderful smells. Some days, he carries a thermos of hollandaise.

Cynthia, Sunday night, is British, and the only one who still likes red meat. She is very tall, fortyish, owns her own travel agency. Lionel tells me she is blue-eyed and freckled and rarely buttons the top two, sometimes three buttons of her silk shirts. She calls him "Pet."

Monday is Marguerite, who never tires of omelets. I know she is blonde, and I picture her barefoot in Capri pants and boat-necked jerseys. Monday is so easy for Lionel, with Marguerite supplying the jumbo eggs and he responsible for the filling alone. She wants to videotape him making an omelet, and I know what she means. Even before his cooking began in earnest, back in our days together of eating steaks and chops and relying heavily on the broiler, Lionel made omelets beautifully.

Kathy, Tuesday, asked chummy, almost conspiratorial questions when she called me to check Lionel's references. "Would you say he is good company?" "Is he discreet?" "Does he buy prime meat?" Her questions caused me pain. I told Lionel that Kathy did not sound bright or independent, did not demonstrate a sense of self, did not seem creative or spontaneous, probably did not have a life of her own to draw upon to enrich the partnership, or, frankly possess any of those qualities he values so dearly in women.

"She has a doctorate," Lionel said.

He accepted Kathy as a client, and we don't discuss her much. I do know that she doesn't own measuring cups or spoons, and that Lionel has to bring his own pepper mill each Tuesday. She is the kind of person who has nothing but ketchup and margarine in her refrigerator and cans of Veg-all on her shelves, yet Lionel describes her as ebullient. She is a teacher, a high school English teacher with a doctorate.

Wednesday is Robin, a graduate of the Harvard Business School. She is short and dark and talkative, but not in the way Lionel likes. Rather than going on and on about his cooking and demanding to know what herb it is that sneaks up on you in the grated zucchini, Robin asks Lionel about his marriage and divorce. She blames her curiosity on her M.B.A. and Harvard's case-study method.

My favorite is Dee-Dee, Thursday, an actuary. Lionel says she is overweight and unattractive. Signing up with Dee-Dee says a lot about Lionel's changing values. Lionel rarely socialized with overweight people, and he never accepted theories about sluggish metabolisms, or childhood fat cells determining adult weight. He always admired concave bellies and the kind of taut upper thighs that seem to be carved from fine-grain wood. To him, such things are effortless.

Dee-Dee talks to Lionel about her problems, and he cheers her up. "I told her my ex-wife has a weight problem, too," he reported pleasantly. "I told her you stir-fry in water now and are down to a size eight."

"Do you discuss my weight with the others?" I ask.

"It doesn't come up," he says.

I know this means that Lionel has not exhausted his list of prepackaged topics: The Summer I Drove a Taxi and Paid Teamster Dues. How Natalie Wood Surprised the *Lampoon* Staff by Showing Up to Accept Her "Worst Actress" Award. Why I Left Law. My Amicable Divorce.

I do not have a weight problem in that version of our life together. I am nearly perfect, a saint. Our divorce was a paragon of civility, no, amiability. We are friends. Better than friends—best friends. We speak to each other frequently. Constantly. We like each other. We love each other in a special way. We never fight. We never fought! Our friends did not take sides. We renewed our symphony seats, our adjacent symphony seats! No children to complicate things. No alimony!

What a wonderful person Lionel appears to be, talking this way about me. He smiles and leans over the table to confide in his audience. He seduces women by radiating such warmth for his ex-wife. He has it all, they think: A fair, generous man. A lean, handsome, educated, single man who speaks of marriage with gusto. A man who remembers to tuck a vanilla bean into his wicker basket to grind with the decaffeinated French roast. No wonder he has a waiting list.

Lionel called me at work and suggested we meet for lunch. He wants me back.

I thought it a little graceless of him to choose the same occasion to describe his latest venture—marketing frozen entrées. He seems to be carried away by the adoration of his harem, and particularly by Robin's B-school thesis on cottage industry. I am tough with him. I predict he will lose his enthusiasm as soon as he gets beyond the glamour of making envelopes of chicken breasts for his Kiev and has to worry about ordering grosses of aluminum plates.

Wanting me back is not out of character for Lionel. His impetuousness is legend in both our families. My mother thinks it may be chemical. No normal person, she says, leaves a job in a distinguished law firm to cook for strangers when he can practically taste an offer of partnership, or throws away a loving wife because of what some magazine multiple-choice test says about The New Fulfillment.

I half expected a reconciliation, the same way I knew Lionel might try out divorce, but his business proposal complicates things. I have to be suspicious: Does he need more cubic feet for freezer lockers and industrial ovens? Does he know something I don't about my building's zoning? Does he want my job skills?

I try not to read too much into his displays of affection for me. When I run into him downtown, and I am with a date, he kisses my cheek, pumps my companion's hand, asks about my father's diabetes, says he will call, kisses me again. My dates are astonished to hear that this prince is my former husband. They spend the rest of the evening counseling me about reconciliation, then never call back. Lionel says he cannot contain his genuine affection for me, that he has become more spontaneous since leaving law and will not be bound by antediluvian rules of etiquette which forbid kissing and fraternizing between former spouses. He is too caught up in the spirit of no-fault.

Over lunch he tells me that "CATERING TO YOU" has not been all fun. He is finding the comparison shopping and menu planning less challenging, and is beginning to cook in large, reheatable quantities. He misses the national news five nights a week. He is on mailing lists for things he never knew existed: equipment that stamps Pennsylvania Dutch designs on pats of butter; fish-of-the-month clubs; edible muffin forms.

Lionel always thinks I want to hear everything—how, because her former husband had a germ phobia, Cynthia rebels by not washing fruit; that Marguerite has taken herself off dairy products for no apparent reason; how Kathy mashes her fish because she is afraid of bones; that Robin has no counter space; that Dee-Dee is not losing weight.

He reaches for my hand and doesn't let go when he orders one slice of marble cheesecake and two black coffees. I know that in another setting, and with a less attentive waitress, Lionel would be outlining the less pragmatic reasons for getting back together.

Lionel insists this lunch is his treat. He walks me back to my office and kisses me in front of my administrative assistant. "I've been thinking it might be fun to have a baby," he calls from the elevator, as its doors glide shut and I wave good-bye.

Lionel gave his clients two weeks' notice and promised to keep in touch through a monthly newsletter. He is going to try restaurant law.

They call sometimes to say hello and ask for recipes. They are dying to hear in my voice a clue about our relationship, which they put to the test by tempting Lionel with free-lance catering jobs. Would he do a cocktail party for twelve? A single moussaka for a potluck brunch?

They call so often, but rarely leave their names. I know them by their questions, and by the longing I hear in their voices.

They'll Smile at You if You're with Me

Tim had studied the rear view for close to a quarter of an hour, admiring the freckled shoulders and the blunt edges of her short blonde hair.

"Fridays are the worst," he said, his opener. "The lines."

She turned to answer, and Tim saw that this new possibility had a large, pregnant belly. *Of course.*

"I know," she said, smiling the relaxed smile of a happily married woman. "Why aren't we all at work where we belong?"

"My license expires today," he said. "Maybe everybody else waited until the last minute."

She put one finger to her lips and leaned closer. "Mine expired yesterday."

Tim admired the front view even more. The short blonde hair was parted in the middle and hooked behind each ear. A tiny pearl sat by itself in the center of each earlobe; the eyes were rusty brown. She leaned over to look at his registry forms. "Timothy Michael McCormick," she read aloud.

He did the same. "Hannah A. Thorson. *Hannah*. You don't hear that one too often."

"I hated it for the first twenty-five years."

Tim took another look at her printed data. "And for the last six?"

She smiled. "Ahh—a mathematician. Now I like it. It's even getting fashionable. People are naming their new babies Hannah."

Better say something, he thought. The line moved forward one applicant. "Is this your first?"

She touched her belly and let her hand rest there. "Sure is."

"That's exciting."

"Do you have any kids?" Hannah asked.

"Not married," said Tim.

She leaned an inch in his direction. By this time they were standing side by side, and their shoulders touched. "Neither am I," she said cheerfully.

They compared photos on their new driver's licenses. "Handsome," she pronounced his.

"Doesn't do you justice," said Tim. He memorized her address before handing it back.

"Well," he said. "I wish you luck with your baby." *Who's the father?*

"Thank you very much," Hannah said. Reluctantly, he thought.

"Would you mind if I called you sometime—see how you're doing?"

"Aren't you nice," Hannah said. Then: "It's not necessary."

"Fine," he said. *They live together, don't believe in marriage, but are committed.* "That's fine. Okay." He took his license from her and put it in his wallet. She murmured good-bye and left.

Wouldn't have worked anyway, Tim thought as he watched tall, blonde Hannah—thin again from the back—weave through the crowd on her way out. Just a nice person; one of those pretty women whose very lack of availability gives them poise.

When she called Tim that night, he had already looked her up in the phone book. He had written down the information and put the slip of paper in his wallet. Things change. In a few years she could be divorced or uncommitted, and he would be just another single guy dating a single mother.

He recognized the voice by its content: "Timothy Michael?" she inquired.

"This is he."

"Hannah Thorson. From the Registry."

He stretched the cord and turned off the television. *Don't get excited. A phone call can mean anything.* "Hi," he managed.

"Are you in the middle of something?"

"No. Just reading. What's up?" *What's up? God.*

"I'm afraid I was rude to you today," Hannah said.

"You were?"

"I think I was. You were very nice about giving me a call sometime. And you probably thought my *no* meant . . . well, *no*."

"True," said Tim.

"The reason I left so fast is that since I've been pregnant—

or actually since I've been showing—no one has said anything like 'can I call you sometime'."

Leave it to me, Tim thought.

"So I got very nervous when you seemed . . ."

"Interested?"

"Interested."

"I see," said Tim. *Here goes*. "Are you involved with the baby's father or anything?"

"I've put you on the spot," Hannah said. "Please don't feel obligated."

"I don't—"

"Let me just say why I called," she continued. "You were very nice this morning, but I don't know what the rules are anymore. I didn't know how to react. Then I felt bad."

"So you're *not* involved with anyone?"

"No."

"Would you like to have dinner Friday night?"

"Out?"

"Whatever."

"I have to warn you. People smile at me all the time. They'll smile at you, too, if you're with me."

"No problem. Do you like Thai food?"

"Sounds great."

Am I crazy? Tim thought. Should I end this before it starts? He connected the voice with the tall, straight torso in front of him in line. The cinnamon eyes. Give or take a few months—his dream woman.

"Where do you live?" he asked, then mouthed the address as she gave it. Before saying good-bye, he asked when the baby was due.

"Three weeks. But first babies are usually late."

"I've heard that," said Tim.

"I'll understand if you change your mind," Hannah said briskly.

"How's seven o'clock?"

"Perfect."

"See you then," said Tim.

"We'll be ready," Hannah said, in her breezy old tone of that morning.

At the agency, Tim told Gary, his co-worker at the next drafting board, about the situation. "Say a guy meets a woman he is really attracted to. . . . They talk and one thing leads to another, and the guy asks her out."

Gary snored and turned back to his pasteup.

"Wait," said Tim. "It gets complicated. Even though this woman is not married and seems to be available—she's very pregnant."

"Bye-bye," Gary said.

"Wait. This is no bimbo unwed mother. This is possibly a woman-of-his-dreams type. Very bright. Friendly. Your basic Cheryl Tiegs."

"Bye-bye," Gary repeated.

"Wouldn't you be curious enough to have dinner with her?"

"How pregnant?"

"Very." Tim outlined a full belly against his own flat one. "A basketball."

Gary shook his head emphatically and pursed his lips.

"You're awfully sure on this one," Tim said. "Not your usual open-minded self."

"This is a textbook *no*. When's the date?"

"Tomorrow night."

"Okay: tomorrow night you pick her up." Gary waved his X-acto knife in the air like a director sketching a scene. "She looks fetching in a madonna-like way. You open the door and she slides into the front seat. The moonlight reflects off her silver-blonde hair and her profile is aglow."

"More yellowish-blonde," said Tim.

"Cut to the restaurant. You have polished off your rack of lamb for two and are sipping an ambitious yet deft Zinfandel. Her story begins . . ." Gary whistled several bars of "Fascination."

"The story," prompted Tim.

"Okay. . . . Many years ago a fabulously wealthy zillionaire, knowing he was about to die, has his sperm frozen at Harvard Medical School. He has no male heir; his daughters are all married to bums—tennis pros and such. From his deathbed, he spots a woman who reminds him of someone he's seen featured in swimsuit issues of *Sports Illustrated.* His butler tracks her down. She agrees to be artificially inseminated with the old guy's frozen spunk and give him an heir. At eighteen, no at *five*, the lad will come into his rightful fortune. Alas, amniocentesis shows she is carrying a female child. She is out. O-U-T. With a small stipend for her troubles."

"Tough," said Tim.

"Wait. Here's where you come in. Did I mention how

lovely she looks in the candlelight? And, with her basketball under the table, how easy it is to imagine her in your arms, white of breast and flat of tummy?"

"Jesus," said Tim, burnishing his layout with unnecessary fervor.

"Want to know how it ends?"

Tim untangled his feet from the rungs of his chair and took refuge in the darkroom.

Hannah invited Tim in for a drink after dinner. Her apartment was the renovated attic of a Victorian house, and was one enormous room with skylights and a gymnasium floor. In one alcove, partially concealed by a lacquered screen, was a crib. Tim looked around for clues—photographs of the father, shaving cream, extra toothbrushes—but the place seemed Hannah's alone. The beer she offered seemed testimony to a male presence, but when it turned out to be imported from Thailand and bought for the occasion, he felt better. Hannah drank milk.

At the restaurant, they had talked about their work. Whenever the waiter appeared, Tim paused; the get-acquainted talk embarrassed him. He had enjoyed walking past the waiting patrons, his hand barely guiding Hannah from behind. He liked being taken for her husband. His smile was an expectant father's—proud and apologetic.

"Where do you work, Timothy?" she had asked as a busboy filled their water glasses.

"A small agency." He checked its effect on the busboy.

Couldn't be more than sixteen, Tim thought. Probably spoke no English.

"I got pregnant on a business trip to Toronto," she announced.

Tim swallowed. "I never asked you what you did."

"Landscape design—mostly commercial."

"No kidding! What have you done around here?"

"The Minuteman Mall?"

"I've never seen it. What else?"

Hannah delivered her list of clients with a wry smile. Hungry for details about her life and insemination, he pumped her instead for professional credits. *Choke.*

At her apartment, Tim tried to concentrate on conversation while Hannah lay on the floor and did exercises for her lower back. Her movements were indiscernible—pelvic tilts, she said, which involved pressing here and relaxing there.

"I just can't get comfortable at this point. Sitting, sleeping, eating . . ."

Tim's sister had gotten puffy-looking with each pregnancy. Ankles, fingers, and face had swelled unappetizingly. Tim had seen his mother, chubby and flushed, in his sister's childbearing face. Not Hannah. She looked like an actress in costume; thin, still lithe, padded with a pillow but otherwise untouched by hormones.

She maneuvered herself onto all fours, inched upwards to her feet, and sat down next to Tim. He crossed and uncrossed his long legs at the ankle; Hannah experimented with different throw pillows at the small of her back. Settled, they smiled.

"So," Tim said.

"Good beer?" she asked.

"Comfortable?" he asked.

"Not your average first date," said Hannah.

Then what in hell did you talk about?" Gary asked Monday.

"Work," said Tim. "She's a designer, too. Landscape."

"So we know she got pregnant in Canada."

Tim frowned. He had been annoyed with himself all weekend. Why hadn't he stayed on the subject: Lovely city, Toronto. Go there often? Drive up and stop at Niagara Falls? Still fuck the father?

"Maybe he's with the Blue Jays," Gary said. "Or the Maple Leafs." He picked up the telephone they shared and propped it up on Tim's board. "Call her. Tell her you're sorry you freaked when she mentioned Toronto."

"I'm such a jerk," Tim muttered. "I started asking her all these stupid questions about her clients."

"What's her number?"

Tim gave the phone back, first checking its underside for stray waxed galleys. "You wouldn't have believed how nice she was. I was practically mute in spots but she never made me feel like I was even a partial jerk."

"She's well brought up. And she's got a lot riding on you."

"I felt her stomach," Tim said after a long silence. "I expected it would be like a big pillow, but it was rock-hard."

Gary trilled in falsetto, "Oh! The baby! Give me your hand. There! Did you feel it?"

"You're quite the asshole sometimes," Tim said. Gary's scenario had not been far off. Hannah had flinched while sitting next to him, and arched her back. "Sometimes she gets me right in the rib cage," she had said.

"She?" Tim had asked.

"She, he. I alternate." Then Hannah had asked Tim if he wanted to feel the baby. He had placed his fingertips tentatively on the crest of her belly. She placed her hand over his, slid it a few inches to the downward slope, and pressed hard. "That's the head, I think."

He had been amazed at what he felt—an actual body, a head. Touching Hannah and her baby had had the effect of a well-timed kiss. They had relaxed. When he said good night—she had walked down the two flights with him—they parted with knowing smiles.

"I'll call her tonight," he told Gary.

There was no answer at 9 P.M. or at the fifteen-minute intervals up to some point during the eleven o'clock news when Tim fell asleep. Shopping, he had first thought. A date? Finally, *Toronto*. He resisted the urge to call in the morning before work, and hoped Gary wouldn't press for a report.

He did.

"I fell asleep," Tim told him. "I'll try tonight." He tried Hannah's apartment during lunch from a phone booth in the lobby of his office building. Her not being there reassured him, somehow, that she wasn't cutting work to rest up from a demanding night of lovemaking. What was the name of her firm? He looked in the Yellow Pages under "landscaping" but saw only ads for gardeners and spring cleanups. He'd call that night.

When there was no answer at her apartment, he set a deadline: no more tries after 11 P.M. He had so little invested in Hannah that he refused to make himself crazy just trying to apologize.

At eleven-thirty, he called hospitals. On his third try, he found her listed.

"What's wrong?" he asked the voice. The line clicked and someone else said, "Patient Information."

"Hannah Thorson," he said hoarsely. A rustle of pages.

"A boy. Six pounds, fourteen ounces."

"When?"

"This morning. Ten-ten."

Tim called Gary.

"Drop it," he said without hesitation. Tim was silent. "Drop it," Gary repeated. "Or stop asking me."

Hannah's phone call woke him before his alarm sounded. He had not been able to fall asleep after getting the news; once he did, he slept fitfully and had unfocused dreams about alternately empty and teeming hospital wards.

"Timothy," she said, her voice a little thick. "I have a son."

"I know," he said, before he thought to act surprised.

"You walk in," Gary said. "There she is, pale but beautiful against crisp white sheets. A child, a tiny helpless infant, suckling at one perfect breast. She looks up at the sound of running shoes squeaking on bare linoleum. Your eyes meet . . ." Out of Gary's pause rose the opening notes of Mendelssohn's wedding march.

Tim usually laughed at Gary's monologues. He tapped his stylus absently on his layout and stared.

"Do me a favor," Gary said. "Get the fuck down there and find out what's going on."

He had to walk past the nursery to get to her room. There were hardly any babies there—one howled noiselessly while another was being changed—and the nurse pointed to a cardboard clock on the wall which announced viewing hours. Tim couldn't see if either was Hannah's.

As soon as he tiptoed into her room, he backed out: a man in a three-piece suit was sitting in a chair next to Hannah's bed.

"Tim!" she called. "It's okay."

The man rose and smiled. There was a stethoscope in his jacket pocket. He patted the edge of her mattress and said, "Keep up the good work."

"Will I see you before I leave?" she asked.

"Nope. Doctor Rosenthal's here tomorrow." Lowering his voice, he said something Tim couldn't hear, then walked out briskly with a professional nod to both.

Hannah grinned. "He said not to have intercourse until my six-week checkup."

"Oh," said Tim.

"Thanks for coming."

I want the truth, he rehearsed. *I have to know the truth. I need the truth.*

"I should have brought flowers," he said, looking around her cramped beige room and seeing none.

Good News

Tim drove home to tell his mother about Hannah in person. Eventually, he knew, it would be regarded as good news.

"I met this wonderful woman, Ma," he would say.

"Who is she?"

"Someone I met at the Registry of Motor Vehicles."

"How long have you known her?"

"Eight days."

She would wipe her hands, palms flat, on her half-apron a few times to collect her thoughts, then ask in her small, polite voice what the girl's name was. Twenty minutes from his mother's house, halfway from his apartment, Tim changed his mind and made an illegal U-turn at the next intersection.

Later, maybe.

He'd bring Hannah with him sometime after she and the

baby came home from the hospital. By then, he could say "a month" when his mother asked how long they'd known each other; or "a long time," and it would be clear that this was not his wishful thinking. A wise move, turning around: Hannah, on paper, would not sound like a match made in any mother's heaven. But in person, in the flesh . . . and Ma so loved new babies, no matter whose they were.

He drove straight to the hospital. A glass case by the elevator displayed stuffed animals on sale in the gift shop. He backtracked to the lobby and bought a fuzzy brown kangaroo, its baby attached by Velcro. The saleslady told him not to worry—there were no buttons or small parts to aspirate.

"There aren't?" said Tim.

"Boy or girl?"

"Boy."

"Is he yours?" the woman asked.

Jesus, he thought, what a question.

"Are you a new daddy?" she tried again in a Kewpie-doll voice that made him realize that she meant "daddy" as opposed to "uncle" or "brother" or "close friend of the parents."

"No, I'm not," Tim said.

Hannah was not in her room, nor was she among the other maternity patients shuffling slowly down the corridor, wincing and pushing their brand-new babies in clear isolettes. "Rooming in," Hannah called it, having selected it like a hotel option, so that she changed and fed Alexander, and swabbed his belly button on her own. The women looked terrible, Tim thought; pale and tired despite the crisp new quilted bathrobes.

Hannah appeared, rounding the corner from the nurses' station. She still had a belly, he noticed, but also the hint of a waistline under her wraparound chenille bathrobe. Its faded blue color, its obvious age and no-nonsense lines made him smile. "Good morning," he called. Hannah walked slowly toward him.

"They don't tell you about this part in childbirth class," she said from a few yards away. She stopped and motioned to him. "Be my cane?"

He took her forearm awkwardly. "I hope it's okay," he said. "My being here before visiting hours."

"They're pretty loose about it. Besides—you could pass for the partner any day." She smiled. " 'The partner' is what they say in birth class instead of 'husband.' Partners can visit round the clock."

Brave Hannah, Tim thought, marching off to birth class alone for all those weeks; *months* for all he knew. Breathing and exhaling with no coach . . . and did they go around the room, the others introducing their husbands and saying how they met? Hannah probably said in her straightforward way, "I got pregnant on a business trip to Toronto. I'm not involved with the father." End of story.

"Should you be on your feet?" he asked.

"It's better than sitting—my episiotomy is killing me."

Episiotomy.

"My stitches. I won't be graphic." She took small sliding steps into the room, her hand clutching Tim's elbow. At her bed, she lowered herself onto her side. Tim didn't know what services to offer.

"Why aren't you at work?" she asked, wincing.

"It's Saturday."

"Sorry. Must be the codeine."

"Is this much pain normal?" asked Tim.

Hannah closed her eyes and nodded.

"Should I get a nurse?"

"No." She studied his face for a minute, then said sadly, "You're very nice."

Oh, no. He'd heard about post-partum depression—women who weep for days and forget to get dressed in the morning.

"What's wrong?" he asked.

She arranged the folds of her bathrobe just so across her knees and didn't answer right away. Tim sat down carefully at the foot of the bed.

"One of us has got to ask if you're already in deeper than you meant to be," she said without looking at him.

"I don't think visiting you in the hospital puts me in deep," said Tim quietly.

"True," said Hannah. "In and of itself. But it's not the same as paying a call on someone who broke her leg after a first date. I had a baby . . . I *have* a baby."

"I know," said Tim.

"And no husband. How do you know that two months, six months, a year down the road you won't say, 'What am I, a social worker? How did I get myself into this?' "

"You really think that'll happen?"

Hannah looked up at the ceiling. "I worked on it last night—the obligatory graceful out."

"It never bothered me that you were pregnant," Tim said,

trying to sound more casual than he felt. "Maybe it helped." He stood and looked down on the roof of the parking garage. Lots of spaces still open. A Mercedes nosed up from a lower level and passed whole empty lanes to park in the farthest corner.

How much could he say—that she was beautiful in a way that other men's beautiful wives were? That he had been relaxed and infinitely more charming when they met in line because she was so obviously unavailable?

"I don't meet women easily," he said, still looking out the window. This is the kiss-off, he thought. Only a sick person would ask a hugely pregnant woman out to dinner and consider it the best date of his life. Hannah knows it. He'd give her the kangaroo and leave.

"I was being mature," Hannah said. "Didn't I say this was my obligatory speech—opening the door for a graceful exit if you're so inclined?"

"I'm not inclined." He walked to the other side of the bed to the visitor's chair and picked up the kangaroo. He held it up and detached the Velcroed baby from the mother's pouch. Hannah laughed aloud, then grimaced.

"The stitches?" She nodded.

"Can't they do anything?"

"I'm getting painkiller every four hours. I also have a hemorrhoid the size of a golf ball from pushing. That doesn't help, either."

"Oh," said Tim. "Should I leave so you can sleep?"

She settled against two stiff pillows and closed her eyes. He was tempted to smooth her hair away from her forehead to elicit a smile, a sign—anything—that would make him feel better. Instead, he left a note propped on her telephone. "Be back tonight. Call me if you need anything. Love, Tim." He worked on the closing, hesitated about the "Love," worried whether it was, from her perspective, an overstatement. He went home to sleep.

The clock said six-thirty when Hannah called and woke him. He was confused by the darkened bedroom and wondered why he had gone to bed on top of the covers with his shoes on.

"Hi," she said. "This is Hannah—Thorson."

Jesus, he thought. *Thorson.* Formal or what?

"I found your note."

"Good," said Tim.

"I wondered if you would mind coming tomorrow instead of tonight?"

"Fine. That's fine. Sure." *Oh, God.*

"Some people from my office want to drop by and see Alexander and you're only supposed to have two guests at a time."

"You could give me a call after they leave and I could run over then," Tim suggested.

"That's sweet, but I'm planning to ask for a sleeping pill and get in a long nap before his midnight feeding."

"Sure," said Tim. "I understand."

"Come anytime tomorrow. Not in the morning, though."

Tim's stomach contracted. This was the kiss-off. "Morning's not good?" he said as casually as he could.

"No. I have breast-feeding class at ten, and they bring lunch around eleven."

Friends from work. That's what she had said. Of course

she'd have friends from work. No reason to think otherwise. Maybe he was just hungry. He'd go out, too—a beer and a bowl of chili at O'Hara's. There were always nice guys at the bar, pretty intelligent guys with interesting problems.

A woman in a furry purple sweater took the stool to his left, and studied the half-dozen offerings on the blackboard. After a few minutes, she asked if she could taste Tim's chili. The bartender brought a clean spoon, which she dipped into his bowl and licked daintily. "Too spicy," she pronounced it. "Thanks anyway." Then she asked if he'd ever had their fish and chips.

"It's good," Tim said.

"Do you know what kind of fish they use?"

Tim shook his head. She asked the bartender, who stared at her unhappily for a few seconds before calling into the kitchen.

"Haddock," yelled a voice from the back.

"One more thing," the woman said, not seeming to notice how conversation at the bar had slowed. "Is it fresh?"

The bartender smiled and checked to see who else was listening. "As fresh as I am," he said.

"I'd like the fish and chips then, with a wedge of lemon and a glass of Chablis."

"You won't be sorry," said the bartender.

Conversation picked up again on either side of Tim and the woman. When she spoke, it was as if their dining partnership was established. "There's no excuse for serving frozen fish in Boston, but I see it all the time. You have to ask. . . . You look very familiar to me," the woman said. "I'm Francine Shapiro."

"I'm here a lot," said Tim. "I like the chili."

"And you are . . . ?"

"Tim McCormick."

"What do you do, Tim?"

"Graphics."

"Does that make you an engineer?" Francine asked.

"No. Designer. I do layouts for ads and brochures and things.

"What about you?" he asked.

"I'm a physical therapist."

He thought he was done with this: Francine conducting her interview in the chatty, self-assured way that women in bars always came on to him. He didn't seem to attract the ones—and he had heard they were out there—who stroked thighs for openers. Francine was asking if he had had to study for a long time to become a graphic designer.

Here's my chance, he thought. Good-bye, Francine Shapiro.

"No," he lied. "I saw an ad on a matchbook cover when I was in trade school."

Her fish and chips arrived soon after, and she swiveled around to face her plate squarely. Tim drank a second beer quickly, and didn't interrupt Francine's conversation with the man on her left to say good-bye.

There were flowers in Hannah's room on Sunday—two big arrangements. One had a toy monkey in its foliage. Buttons for eyes, he noticed.

"Pretty flowers," he said, but not right away.

"Paul and Dana brought them last night."

"Your co-workers?"

Hannah nodded. "And you'll never guess who the other's from."

Oh, no? "Toronto?"

Hannah shook her head, dismissing the guess as if it had no more significance than a name picked from a phone book. "He doesn't know. They're from my parents!"

"I didn't think of that," Tim said.

"I can't believe it. It's practically an endorsement. Read the card."

Tim pulled the small rectangle from its envelope. The design was awful: a little naked boy in cowboy boots with a holster hiding his private parts. *Dear Hannah, Our best wishes to you and your son. Mother and Dad.*

"I guess that's nice," Tim said.

"It's a white flag. They were *not* pleased about my pregnancy."

"How did they find out he was born?"

"I left a message with my father's answering service. I hardly expected to hear from them, though."

"That's great," said Tim.

"Wait, there's more. I called to thank them for the flowers, and Mother said they'd been doing a great deal of soul-searching, and wanted me to move home until I got back on my feet."

"Home," Tim repeated. "I see."

"It's just a grand gesture. I'm sure they thought I'd never accept."

"Did you?"

"It's almost tempting. Just for a few weeks."

Don't, Tim thought. "I can help you out with stuff around the house . . . grocery shopping," he offered. "Besides, you won't always feel as sore as you do now."

"We'll see," she said.

"How long would you stay?"

"I get six weeks' maternity leave."

"Maybe your mother would come here for a week or so. My mother did that when my sister had her kid."

"She's not the type," Hannah said grimly. "In the best of circumstances. Essentially, she's offering me room and board and Fanny, the housekeeper."

"It doesn't sound so great," Tim said. Six weeks, he thought. That would be the end of it. One date and several hospital visits were not sufficient grounds for writing and calling her in Minnesota. Her parents would find such attentiveness unhealthy. He needed time. He needed her to say no.

Alexander nursed with a rhythmic drone that amazed Tim and made Hannah laugh. His little head looked bald from a distance but was actually covered with a white-blonde fuzz.

Here I am, thought Tim, watching Hannah take her breast out of her nightgown and put it in her son's mouth. Just like that. I am watching nonchalantly, the way a true partner would, even though it is an amazingly beautiful breast and this is our first sexual contact.

Every few minutes Hannah laughed as Alexander lost his way and nuzzled frantically. "He looks like one of those blind baby mice rooting around for its mother," she said.

"He's cuter than a baby mouse," said Tim.

"He is pretty cute, isn't he?"

"He looks just like you."

Hannah smiled down at her son.

"Don't you think so?" Tim prompted.

"It's hard to tell this early."

Here goes. "What does his father look like?"

Hannah narrowed her eyes and hunched her shoulders. "Horns. A long tail . . . pitchfork." She leaned back against the pillows and laughed. Alexander lost his hold and squealed.

"I'm serious," said Tim.

Hannah slapped her cheek in self-reproof. "What do you want to know?"

"Who is he?"

"Jeremy Coombs. Age forty-something. Civil servant. Blue eyes, gray hair. . . . A pleasant interlude in an otherwise boring business trip. Will that do?"

"Does he know he has a son?"

"No need for that," said Hannah.

"Maybe he'd want to marry you," Tim ventured.

"I don't want to marry him," she answered.

Be cool, Tim thought. Don't look too relieved.

"See," said Hannah. "The devil you know, right?"

Tim smiled. *Gray hair.*

The pediatrician was a young woman with a long red braid and a hyphenated name. She said Alexander was thriving. It was obvious to Tim she had read Hannah's chart and knew her social history: there was no Mommy-Daddy talk and no attempt to draw Tim into the conversation. Hannah and the doctor discussed feeding on demand, Alexander's bilirubin count, and brands of breast pumps.

"Have you thought about circumcision?" the doctor asked next.

"Not much," said Hannah. "Should I?"

"We'd do it before you take him home, so I'd like to know as soon as possible."

"Whatever's best for him," said Hannah.

Dr. Freedman-Levy moved from a chair to the edge of Hannah's bed. "We don't recommend it anymore for medical purposes, so the factors are religious and social."

"Social?" Hannah repeated.

"Some feel that a little boy's penis should be the same as his father's, or the male figure in his life . . . which is to say, his *mother's* life."

Here it is, thought Tim. He raised his glance up from a spot on the linoleum to look at Hannah, who sat cross-legged on the bed, limber at last. She leaned sideways for a clearer view around the doctor.

"Timothy?" she asked lightly, business as usual; but her eyes, he thought, I'm pretty sure her eyes know what she's asking.

Baby's First Christmas

Hannah has stopped thinking of Jeremy Coombs in a romantic context, stopped splicing him into poignant reunion scenes. Rather, she imagines a lunch meeting where she informs the impeccably dressed, slightly impatient Canadian civil servant that she has had a son by him.

"It happened, of course, the week of our conference in Toronto," she would explain. "Alexander has your mouth and chin, and presumably your blood type because he doesn't have mine. I don't want anything. I am telling you because it is the right thing to do."

Her projections are entirely natural, she tells herself, and carry no suggestion of love or lust. Jeremy is, after all, present in the lines and planes of Alexander's face—a biological fact of life. And what's the harm? She is certainly not going to call and startle him with the news of the baby's existence, especially since she's never heard a word since the conference. Hannah is not a dreamer. Jeremy Coombs has his own life, sons and a wife in Toronto.

Her parents say she's a foolish girl: it's all very well, noble actually, to support and raise a son alone, but quite idealistic. The Canadian (all along Hannah's refused to tell them his name) should pay for Alexander's housing, food, clothing, and education, the Thorsons maintain. Consequently, Hannah has set ground rules for her Christmas visit to her parents. They are not to badger her about paternal responsibilities or play guessing games about their grandson's chromosomes. Hannah's mother has begun to refer to the father as "Anonymous." Her daughter hears in it a twist of irony or acceptance, which she thinks is a good sign. Neither parent likes to talk about what must have taken place between Hannah and the Canadian—what led up to their daughter's pregnancy besides the obvious. Mrs. Thorson likes to speculate aloud in an *entre-nous* fashion about the Attraction they must have felt toward each other.

"Mother," Hannah says, annoyed, "I obviously slept with the man. Are you looking for reassurances that I was so consumed by burning desire that I couldn't help myself?"

"Don't patronize me," Mrs. Thorson says. "I thought we had the kind of relationship where I could ask you a personal question without your biting my head off. Evidently, I was wrong."

This is an effective tactic. Hannah doesn't like to hear that cold edge in her mother's voice.

"Anything you tell me will not be repeated to your father," Mrs. Thorson coaxes.

Hannah thinks for a minute. She probably can discuss with equanimity Jeremy's failure to call, write, or in any way acknowledge their four days in Toronto. She is quite sure she no longer feels anything for Jeremy Coombs; she knows he is beneath contempt for the way he handled their affair. The only reason she doesn't write him off as a totally worthless human being is because once, for four days, she thought so completely otherwise, and because his character genes are inside Alexander.

Now she is being asked to discuss the Night and the Spark. "It was one of those things," she tells her mother.

Mrs. Thorson nods eagerly. Hannah sees questions about his height, looks, lineage, occupation, and religion hovering on her mother's lips. Enough coziness, she decides. I should never have let her open this door.

"What if," her mother says, meeting the silence head on, "your telephone rang one day and it was Alexander's father. Would you say something about the baby?"

Hannah has imagined such a long-distance call from Jeremy. Her tactic, she had decided many times over, would be to exchange pleasantries, inquire as to the nature of his call, confirm his business address, and tell him she'd be in touch. She would have her attorney draft a letter informing Jeremy of his son's existence, but asking for nothing. It would be marked "personal and confidential" so his secretary wouldn't open it, and he would appreciate her discretion. Then, when Alexander was older and wanted to trace his roots, they could contact him without fear that the shock would kill a by then aging Jeremy Coombs.

"He won't call," Hannah says. "Why should I waste my time on conjecture?"

"What I don't understand," Mrs. Thorson continues, "is how a man could fall in love with someone, then disappear from sight as if nothing had happened. The only conclusion I can come to is that he was married." Her deduction is announced in the manner of an unwitting TV detective, solving tonight's episode.

Hannah stares at her mother's triumphant face. "Of course he's married," she says evenly. "What did you think?"

"Married," Mrs. Thorson repeats softly. "I see." After a long silence she asks if Hannah knew it at the time.

"He told me he was separated. But that's neither here nor there."

"Not entirely," her mother says. "'Separated' is like 'divorced' in some situations. Marriages can be completely over, for years and years—irreconcilable—when people are separated."

"I'm assuming he lied, Mother. His wedding ring was probably in his shirt pocket the whole time. Some men are chronically separated at conferences."

"But you don't know anything for sure?"

"You know what you're doing, don't you?" Hannah asks. "You're convincing yourself that he's honorable, single—wondering how to get in touch with that Thorson woman from the States so he can ask her out for a date like a proper gentleman. Or ask for her hand."

"I am not," Mrs. Thorson protests.

"Maybe he's had amnesia all this time. . . . I like that: *amnesia*. In a tropical hospital somewhere with a ceiling fan . . . murmuring my name."

Mrs. Thorson doesn't smile.

"Let's drop it," Hannah says.

"I have one more thing to say," her mother continues, "if you'll allow me this—what if something happened to you? Who would take care of Alexander? Your father and I won't be around forever. Who would do it—your friends from the office?"

"No," Hannah says.

"You've thought about it, then?"

"Only an imbecile wouldn't have thought about it."

"Don't be short with me," her mother says.

"Well, just rest assured I've thought about it."

"And concluded . . . ?"

Who? Hannah thinks, who would do this for me? Jeremy? She imagines sad, orphaned Alexander—Paddington Bear with a tag around his neck—boarding an Air Canada flight to meet the biological father he never knew.

No. *Who?* She gives the answer before thinking it through, before anticipating their questions. "Timothy McCormick," Hannah enunciates, as if it's written somewhere official and notarized.

"I was dating him when I had Alexander," Hannah explains to both parents that night. They are eating at one end of the large dining room table. Fanny has prepared the meal and left for the day, and Alexander is asleep in Hannah's old crib.

"Should I assume this is not the fellow who got you pregnant?" Mr. Thorson asks.

"I was already pregnant when we met. We had our first date a few nights before my water broke."

Mr. and Mrs. Thorson both pause in their eating. "What is his understanding of your circumstances?" Mr. Thorson asks.

"Oh," says Hannah airily, "you know . . . modern woman elects single parenthood." She takes a sip of wine, swallows, and smiles challengingly.

"I know you delight in shocking us," her mother says. "But we're modern people. It doesn't work."

"This has been going on for . . . ?"

"Since September."

Mr. Thorson raises his voice. "You're talking about some suitor as Alexander's guardian, someone you met a few months ago? Am I missing something here?"

Mrs. Thorson touches her mouth with precise dabs of a linen napkin. "Why would he do it for you," she asks, measuring each word, "if you're not even married to the man?"

Hannah takes a bite of meat. Fanny's wonderful stuffed breast of veal. She chews slowly and takes a sip of wine before answering. "It's hard to explain," she begins.

"He's the father, isn't he?" Mr. Thorson says. "This Canada business is just a red herring, am I right?"

"*No*. I met Tim at the Registry of Motor Vehicles. We were renewing our licenses. Anyway, we established a friendship fairly fast, then I had Alexander. He was wonderful to me."

"Are you in love with the man?" Mrs. Thorson asks.

Her husband glares at his wife, his daughter, his plate, and back to his daughter. "She'd better be," he growls.

Mr. Thorson has left for the day by the time Hannah comes downstairs for breakfast. Her mother is alone in the kitchen. "Don't worry," she sings out as soon as Hannah appears. "No questions, no maternal advice."

"Good."

She asks if Hannah wants eggs—she's been scrambling theirs with fresh basil and it's delicious . . . a restaurant downtown did it at a brunch and she guessed the secret ingredient.

"Fine," says Hannah.

Her mother breaks the eggs expertly with one hand and scrambles them with a whisk. "Lots of fresh-ground pepper and a little Parmesan, too," she instructs over her shoulder. "The basil grows beautifully on the windowsill this time of year."

"I'll try it," Hannah says.

"It's lovely for a late-night supper, too. After the theater or something like that."

Hannah laughs. Mrs. Thorson arches her eyebrows.

"You have an exalted view of my social life," Hannah explains. "Most nights I eat standing at the kitchen sink."

Her mother is silent as she cooks. Hannah wonders if she should reassure her that it was hyperbole; that, in fact, she has friends and evenings out. Mrs. Thorson refills her own coffee cup and sits down with Hannah after serving the eggs.

"Do you ever see him?"

"Who?"

"The father."

"Oh, God," says Hannah.

Mrs. Thorson makes a fist and hits the table with a restrained thump. "This is unbearable," she says. "As a mother I have to say this is unbearable."

Hannah takes a bite and ignores the outburst. "Delicious. Thank you."

"Indulge me," Mrs. Thorson says. "Call this man; find out if he is married or if he wants a stake in this. At least we'll know what we're up against. I'll leave you alone after that."

"No," says Hannah.

"I'll call. I'll ask for the lady of the house."

Hannah groans. "Talk about clichés."

"Well, what if I make up a plausible reason for calling—like a market research survey . . . or that I'm looking for an old school chum?"

"I'll leave," Hannah says. "I swear to God I'll pack us up and leave on the next flight."

Mrs. Thorson doesn't retreat. "You are thirty-one years old. You have an infant and no husband. . . . I don't even know if this new boyfriend of yours has a car to meet you at the airport."

Hannah stands up and carries her dirty plate to the sink. She washes it and doesn't speak until the water is turned off. "I might call him this spring," she tells her mother.

She parks her father's car as close to the phone booth as she can, in order to have an unobstructed view of Alexander as she talks. He is asleep in his carseat, peaking out from a woolly cocoon of knitted gifts. The number is in her address book, written confidently in ink the last night of the conference.

She dials, turning her head every few numbers to check the car. "Jeremy Coombs," Hannah says to the woman who answers the Ministry phone.

"May I say who's calling?"

"Washington."

After a long pause, the woman comes back on the line and says that Mr. Coombs is in a meeting, and could he return the call presently?

"No," says Hannah. "Put me through."

He answers with a "Coombs here."

"It's not Washington," she says. "It's Hannah Thorson."

"Clever girl," he says. "How are you?"

"Very well."

"And how's the work going?"

"Fine. I'm a partner now."

"Lovely!"

"And I have a son."

"I'm *so* pleased," he says automatically.

"He was born September eighteenth—"

"Lovely," Jeremy repeats.

Hannah speaks slowly. "I know there are people in the room with you, but you can do the arithmetic when you're alone."

There is a pause, then: "How nice that you called."

"I won't do it again," she says and hangs up first.

Tim picks up when he hears Hannah's voice beginning a message on his answering machine. "I'm here," he interrupts.

"Working?"

"Just trimming galleys."

"Merry Christmas," Hannah says.

"You sound terrible," Tim says. "Are they driving you crazy?"

Hannah makes a strangled noise in her throat, then laughs.

"What did they say about the little guy?" Tim asks.

"A fine lad," Hannah says in a flat voice.

"Didn't they think he was incredibly cute?"

"Think? Maybe. *Say?* No."

"I really miss him," Tim says. "I miss both of you."

"Two more days."

"Did Alex get excited when he saw the Christmas tree?" Tim asks.

Hannah laughs. "It's all he talks about."

"You know what I mean—the way his eyes bug out?"

"Sort of."

"I hope you're taking pictures."

"Baby's First Christmas," Hannah intones.

Her father drives them to the airport the day after Christmas. "Parents want certain things for their children," he says. "Certain basic things which make us appear quite conventional. Particularly where daughters are concerned. And I don't think all parents would have taken your situation so well."

"I know that," says Hannah.

"I'm not patting myself on the back. I'm saying maybe we don't always get credit for being as liberal-minded as we've been."

"Did I say anything?" Hannah asks.

"Yes, you did. Several things about *this* young man and *that* young man, and the mysterious Canadian . . . all very light-hearted, as if getting married and giving Alexander a name is against your religion."

"Not at all," says Hannah.

"Some parents with the means might have hired a detective, you know."

Hannah answers with a derisive laugh. "And some daughters might have cheered them on from the sidelines."

He smiles faintly. "Not you, though."

They drive in silence until they reach the turnoff for the airport. "I called him," Hannah tells her father. "For the record."

"And?"

"And"—she mimics his courtroom tone—*"now . . . he . . . knows."*

Mr. Thorson shakes his head wearily. "I don't suppose you got careless and left a record of his number on my phone bill?"

"Are you kidding?" Hannah asks.

She insists he not bother parking, but drop them at the

terminal. They kiss good-bye on the curb after he unloads Hannah's suitcases from the trunk of the Mercedes and attracts a porter without a gesture.

"You can tell Mother I called him, as long as she understands that's the end of it," Hannah says.

"Son of a bitch," he murmurs.

Hannah leans into the back seat and brings forth Alexander. His arms, in a stiff blue cotton snowsuit, stick straight out from his body. His eyes look wide and amazed. Hannah laughs aloud, amazed herself that this is why they're cursing Jeremy Coombs.

The Day Woman

Dr. Freedman-Levy said that Alexander would get every ear infection and every gastrointestinal bug passing through a day-care center, and was it possible to hire a woman to come in?

Hannah answered child-care ads in the "Situations Wanted" column of the Sunday *Globe* and the suburban weeklies. The women who had drivers' licenses and good grammar specified "no infants," and the ones who would take Alexander sounded like losers in a variety of ways. So Hannah advertised: "Single wrkg. mother sks. loving care in home for infant. References." The only call was from another single mother who proposed they live together and share the babysitting. Hannah *did* have a house, didn't she?

"Only a one-bedroom apartment," Hannah lied. After hanging up, she found herself visualizing the caller in tight hip-hugger jeans and stringy hair, phoning from her subsidized housing unit. "Single mother" sat badly even with Hannah. She revised her ad, with good results. "Landscape architect seeks loving care in home, days, for beautiful infant boy" brought many responses. Five showed up for interviews. Hannah hired Mrs. Pelletier, dressed in a nurse's uniform and thick-soled white shoes, the only applicant whose arms floated out to Alexander when Hannah presented him ceremoniously. Her references said she didn't watch daytime television, and liked to iron while the baby napped; in her last position, she had alphabetized the bottles on the spice rack one rainy afternoon.

Hannah's parents were delighted to hear she had engaged a day woman. Their murmurings about how good it was for Hannah to be back in her professional milieu were interpreted by Hannah to mean, "Maybe you'll meet someone now." They sent her three expensive dresses from a new shop in Minneapolis specializing in executive women's wear. The card said, "To gild our lily. Knock 'em dead. All exchangeable. Mother and Father." They enclosed small, appropriate gifts for Mrs. Pelletier—candy and stationery—but nothing for their grandson. He doesn't know the difference, Hannah told herself; when he's old enough they will.

"I should have the father's number at work in case there's an emergency and I can't reach you," Mrs. Pelletier suggests the first morning she arrives.

"He's too far away to be of any help," Hannah tells her.

"Of course," the nurse answers.

When Hannah returns from work, there is another question: Did Mr. and Mrs. Thorson's custody arrangement ever involve weekdays, and should she plan her vacations accordingly?

No, Hannah says. They never involve weekdays.

Possibly when Alexander is older and has school vacations, Mrs. Pelletier suggests.

Alexander's father and I are not divorced.

We were never married.

I understand, Mrs. Pelletier says, too quickly for Hannah to believe her.

"I wanted a child," Hannah feels compelled to say. "I was thirty and didn't know if I'd ever get married. I thought it would be worth whatever I'd have to go through not to miss this."

Or maybe I fell in love on a business trip, and didn't think I needed that morning refill of spermicide in my diaphragm.

"Do you have any children?" Hannah asks Alexander's nurse.

"One." Mrs. Pelletier smiles briefly.

"Then you know," says Hannah.

Three weeks later she calls Mrs. Pelletier from the office and asks if she could possibly stay an extra two hours.

"Working late?" she asks. *Drinks with a client on my time?* her tone implies.

"I'm over my head," says Hannah. *Why am I lying?* she wonders.

"I like twenty-four hours' notice, especially for a Friday night."

"Can you do it?"

"As it happens, yes."

"How's my guy?" Hannah asks.

Mrs. Pelletier's voice warms noticeably. "An angel."

"Kiss him for me," Hannah tells her, then grimaces at the thought of the nurse's thin pursed lips.

Over an early dinner, Elliot says he'd like to see this kid of hers, and points out that the nurse is an *employee* of Hannah's, not her housemother.

"I don't think she's thrilled with my marital status," Hannah explains. "Bringing home a date would only call attention to it."

"I repeat: an *employee*."

"Another time," says Hannah.

"'Good help is hard to find'?"

"Exactly," says Hannah. "Besides, I implied I was working late."

Elliot leans back in his chair and smiles coolly. "Kind of like sneaking around in high school, isn't it?"

"No, it's not," says Hannah. "It took my entire maternity leave to find someone good."

Elliot shakes his head impatiently. "I'd give her an extra few bucks for tonight and forget about it."

He doesn't have a clue, Hannah thinks. *Dating*. "I really should get home," she tells him.

"Another time?" he asks.

"Lunch is good any day," Hannah answers.

He picks up the check and studies it for an overly long time. "Seventeen apiece with tip," he says finally.

Mrs. Pelletier opens the front door with a screaming Alexander in her arms. Hannah takes him and struggles to unbutton her silk blouse and free a breast.

"It's almost like he could tell time," Mrs. Pelletier says when the baby's sobs have turned into noisy gulps. "Come six o'clock he refuses a bottle! He's a smart one, all right. He knew it was time for his titty."

It's all my fault, Hannah thinks. She had risen during dinner to call home, but logical Elliot had talked her out of it. "Either he'll be fine, in which case we'll finish our meal. Or he'll be crying, in which case we'll finish our meal," he had said. The experienced father of two; only on alternate weekends now, but he remembers all the tricks.

Hannah rests her lips on Alexander's brow. "Mama's sorry," she murmurs, trying not to cry.

"He knew, all right," Mrs. Pelletier repeats.

Hannah moves to the living room couch with her son cradled in her arms. His eyes are closed and his chin is pumping reflexively. "I think he was more tired than hungry," Hannah whispers. "He doesn't know how to go to sleep without the breast, so he was getting frantic."

"That's what I thought," Mrs. Pelletier says.

"He wouldn't take the frozen?"

"It didn't smell right when I defrosted it."

Hannah sighs and rubs the white-blonde fuzz on his head with the tip of one finger. She looks up to see Mrs. Pelletier studying her with an almost sympathetic expression.

"You'll get your work done," says the nurse. "They shouldn't ask you to work on a Friday night—a woman with a young baby. Can't you tell them you'll take work home and catch up on the weekends?"

Weekends. Hannah imagines tonight's welcome-home scene through dapper Elliot's eyes: baby hysterical; me clawing at my executive separates to free a breast. How to Test a Date's Paternal Quotient and Guarantee Most Never Return. Mrs. Pelletier shrugs into her coat. "Next Friday night I have a commitment," she tells Hannah.

Mrs. Thorson calls late Saturday night and wakes Hannah. Her voice is animated and confiding as if she's swept in from a party and perched on her daughter's bed.

"Remember Lanning Fredericksen?" she asks.

"Sure," says Hannah.

"I spent the whole night talking to his mother at the Rasmussens'."

"That's nice."

"Guess where he is!"

"Boston, Massachusetts," Hannah says without inflection.

"You know what she said to me? 'Lanning's been in love with Hannah since he was twelve years old. He still asks about her.' I told her you were an architect in Cambridge and unattached, and she was tickled pink."

"Oh?"

"Lanning's single, too. And ripe, from what she told me. Not having an easy time meeting the right kind of woman."

"You told her about Alexander, I assume."

Mrs. Thorson pauses. "Not in so many words."

"Why spoil a nice conversation, right?"

"I'm sorry," her mother says briskly. "I was calling with what I thought was an interesting lead. I'd rather this didn't turn into a debate."

Hannah knows her mother will not soften unless coaxed. "Tell me what he's doing in Boston," she prompts.

"Teaching . . . at the Harvard Business School!"

"Christ."

"Edith said he was always a good student, just didn't test well. Apparently he blossomed at the U. of M.—Phi Bete, everything."

"He never struck me as having anything on the ball," says Hannah.

"Which one *was* he? I couldn't get a clear picture in my mind."

"Tall, stoop-shouldered, goofy-looking? Dave Davidson's sidekick?"

Mrs. Thorson is silent, remembering. "Maybe it was Dave Davidson I was picturing," she says slowly. "Did you go to a prom with him in white piqué?"

"Junior year."

Hannah's mother is silent again. "It's funny, because Edith has a horsey face, and even as we were talking I was picturing that handsome Dave and looking for a resemblance. . . ."

"Oh, well," Hannah says happily. "Back to the drawing board."

"Nonsense. I gave Edith your phone number to pass on to him. . . . How bad can he be if he teaches at Harvard Business School?"

Hannah laughs.

"One date, for God's sake. He'll take you to dinner. You have to eat anyway."

Okay, Hannah thinks, Alexander comes, too.

Lanning telephones the next day and does not sound goofy except for his initial insistence that she guess who he is. He is eager to see her and to talk about the old crowd. Can she believe they've been in the same city for ten years and not run into each other? "Let's have dinner," he says confidently, intimately: *Let's close the deal.* He names a time and place that are too late and too chic for a baby in a Snugli. Hannah says yes.

A man that could be Lanning smiles pleasantly at Hannah as she enters the restaurant with Alexander over her shoulder. It could be he, she thinks, rendered almost distinguished by male-pattern baldness and a ginger-colored beard. "Lanning?" she says.

His smile freezes when he realizes this woman and baby are his date.

Hannah extends her free hand to shake his. "He should sleep the whole time. I just nursed him in the car."

"Did you bring your husband, too?" he asks.

"I would if I had one," says Hannah.

A waiter leads them to a remote table by the kitchen, and helps Hannah snap Alexander into a Snugli. "My mother didn't say anything about a baby," he says when they are alone.

"That's because *my* mother didn't say anything about a baby."

"She doesn't know?" he asks.

Hannah laughs, then leans over the table conspiratorially. "No one knows. You're the very first. My parents would have made me give him up."

"Jesus," says Lanning.

"So I just kept letting the seams out on my clothes. They never noticed."

Lanning stares down at the patch of scalp sticking out of the Snugli. "I don't know what to say: 'Congratulations' or 'I'm sorry'?"

"Why would you say 'I'm sorry'?" Hannah asks.

Lanning shrugs. "It doesn't sound like much fun."

"Oh, I see," says Hannah, her brow furrowed as if grappling with his logic. "I might not have known there were alternatives, so the mere fact that I have a baby doesn't necessarily mean I wanted one? Something like that?"

"I didn't mean to insult you, Hannah."

"'Congratulations' will do fine."

"Congratulations," says Lanning without enthusiasm.

Too late, thinks Hannah.

Mrs. Thorson is not amused when Lanning's mother calls, all solicitude, and asks oblique questions about Hannah's last twelve months. "I finally said, 'Edith, is there something Lanning wants to know about Hannah that he can't ask her himself?' As it turns out, the woman is calling to break the news because Lanning told her we didn't know about Alexander."

"Boy," says Hannah. "What a big-mouth."

"In other words, you didn't like him and decided to amuse yourself through dinner by fabricating a Little Matchgirl story?"

"It wasn't premeditated. He had such a Harvard Business School reaction to Alexander that I couldn't help myself."

"Tell me the truth," her mother says. "Did you breast-feed the baby at the table?"

"I didn't have to — his mere existence offended Lanning."

"You expect people to learn about the baby and have no reaction at all other than admiration, don't you? No one's allowed to be practical; your father and I learned that months ago — don't ask mundane things like how you're going to manage, or why you did it .... Some terribly nice man who's been infatuated with you since childhood wants to take you out and you cut him dead — "

"And God knows I'm hardly in a position where I can afford to be choosy... "

There is an angry pause before Mrs. Thorson says, "I can't talk to you."

"I don't need to be patronized by Lanning Fredericksens," says Hannah.

"Fine."

"Besides, you thought you were marrying me off to Dave Davidson. You can't be too disappointed about Lanning."

Mrs. Thorson doesn't answer.

"Tell me the truth," Hannah tries, "do you want your next grandchild to have a horse face?"

"Very funny," her mother says, meaning the joke has registered against her will.

"I didn't know he'd go running to his mother," says Hannah.

Hannah brings home a take-out pizza and tells Mrs. Pelletier that even a small pie takes her two nights to eat. Will she stay for supper and save her from reheated pizza tomorrow?

Maybe one slice, says the nurse.

It seems impertinent to ask if anyone's waiting at home, so Hannah says, "Feel free to eat and run if you have plans for the evening."

"Just my programs," says Mrs. Pelletier.

Hannah is happy to have a conversational seed to sow. "Which programs?" she asks enthusiastically.

"'All My Children,' 'One Life to Live,' and 'General Hospital,'" says Mrs. Pelletier. "I tape them on my VCR."

"Well," says Hannah. "And you watch them at night! What a good idea." *Truly pathetic.*

"I usually don't admit it," says the nurse. "It makes a bad impression."

"Nonsense," says Hannah.

"At least at night it's my own time to waste. I relax."

"Do you fast-forward during the commercials?" asks Hannah.

"When I think of it," says Mrs. Pelletier.

Hannah pinches the melted cheese off her slice and takes bites between questions. "Do you live alone?" she asks.

"Yes."

"Mr. Pelletier passed away?"

The nurse answers matter-of-factly. "A long time ago. Before my daughter was born."

"That must have been awfully hard for you."

"I raised my daughter alone," says Mrs. Pelletier. "Like you're doing."

Except, Hannah thinks: widow; *legit.*

"Except," says Mrs. Pelletier, "you have that nice family behind you."

"I wouldn't go that far," says Hannah. "More like, how could you do this to us? What should we tell our friends?"

"Still," says Mrs. Pelletier, "they talk to you. They send you presents."

"They've come around," Hannah says. "But you have to understand what I'm up against. My mother's wedding dress is stuffed with tissue paper and wrapped in plastic, waiting for me. It's been standing up in a guest room closet since I can remember."

Mrs. Pelletier chews a bite of pizza slowly, and studies Hannah. "You do have those looks," she says, "those bridal magazine looks."

Hannah rolls her eyes.

"You'll have chances," says Mrs. Pelletier. "Even I had chances when I was your age."

"But . . . ?" Hannah asks.

Mrs. Pelletier shakes her head.

"Not the right person?"

"I didn't think so at the time."

At the time.

Hannah imagines her mother sitting with them, sending

discreet signals to her daughter. *See.* See what you'll be if you keep saying no? She didn't think so *at the time.* Need I remind you: Elliot, Lanning . . . Timothy?

"You'll come out all right," Mrs. Pelletier continues. "The baby won't matter to them—to the boyfriends. Or even to their parents. And no one will put a label on Alexander, either. It's a different world nowadays, thank goodness." She squares her shoulders as if returning to her normal, unconfiding state. "I'll take a second piece after all," she says.

Hannah thinks: Should I back this up a few sentences and ask a direct question—was there ever a wedding or a Mr. Pelletier?

But Mrs. Pelletier has moved on, cutting her second slice into bite-size pieces with a plastic knife and fork.

Projection, Hannah thinks. This is a pep talk, not a confession. All she meant was, "I watch soap operas; I know all about modern romance. I've seen this happen in the nicest families."

Later, watching television alone, Hannah wonders, what do I do at night that's so enviable? Two newspapers; cocoa in my Mount Holyoke tenth-reunion mug. Network news. Bed.

She falls asleep planning: Apologize to Mother for bringing the baby on my date. . . . Buy Elliot lunch. . . . See how Tim is.

By daylight the resolutions seem excessive. Instead, Hannah thinks, I will not buy a VCR. I will keep the phone plugged in at night. When it rings I will answer it.

Land of the Midnight Sun

Tim keeps track of Hannah's age and her baby's, and although he has not seen either of them for two years and several months, he knows she will be thirty-four in May, and Alexander three in September. He reads the wedding and engagement announcements in two Sunday papers for any changes, and periodically dials Directory Assistance to make sure they're still there. One day he will call them.

They broke up, Tim has always thought, for a stupid reason: Hannah's preoccupation with not being able to love him as much/deeply/unconditionally as he loved her. A nonissue, he argued; if *he* didn't mind being less loved, wasn't that his prerogative?

Gary still thinks she'll be back; "crawling back" is what he actually says. On her hands and knees. His stated goal is to make his friend strong enough or angry enough, or in love with someone else enough, to say no to Hannah when her phone call comes.

He and Tim no longer work together—Gary has moved up to head another agency's art department, and Tim designs college catalogues on his own—but they share the first floor of a two-family house. Tim asked Gary to be his roommate as soon as Hannah ended things. Gary said no several times before announcing at lunch one day that he was almost certainly gay and didn't think, under the circumstances . . .

"Why not?" Tim had said out of loyalty and loneliness; embarrassed, too, for not picking up something so important on his own. Once agreed, they discussed the positive side of what Gary called bisexual housing: they would not be in competition for lovers and there would be a clinical detachment with which to see romantic trouble spots in each other's lives.

"I dated women for a long time," said Gary. "Some of my best friends are women. I love them."

"You always helped me," Tim agreed.

In more than two years of living together, Gary has brought home many women for Tim. The fact that none has worked out, Tim figures, is that women who are drawn to Gary's extravagant personality are not sidetracked by low-key roommates.

"Tim likes women he can worship," Gary says when introducing a particularly pretty new acquaintance to his roommate. "And *she* likes the mature boy-next-door type. So here. Fall in love." The woman laughs, flattered, and makes conversation for a short time; humors him, Tim thinks, the way girlfriends of old fraternity brothers made a point of being nice to the unattached guys.

"The young ones like you," Gary instructs Tim. "You're not threatening, and you're cute." This conversation usually takes place at breakfast after Tim has returned empty-handed the night before. Tim doesn't tell Gary he is not interested in the young ones. If he confesses to liking women thirty-fourish, and blonde in a no-nonsense way, Gary starts his harangue about getting over Hannah.

It's still a painful subject, and Tim wonders if he'll ever be cured. He joined a group organized by his health plan for the divorced, separated, and broken-hearted, but dropped out halfway through. People didn't know what to say when he explained how he'd met Hannah, how she was nine months pregnant and he didn't care. The group leader called him at home after that session to say that the health plan did approve private short-term therapy in certain cases and that he would be happy to set the wheels in motion.

"Listen," Tim explained. "I met this beautiful woman in line at the Registry of Motor Vehicles and I couldn't tell from behind that she was pregnant. That doesn't make me a sick person."

It became clear that his fellow members were dying to know the rest of the story. "Have you always been attracted to pregnant women?" a fat, divorced nurse asked him with psychiatric detachment.

"She called *me,*" he said.

"Why?" a few voices asked.

"I don't know. We had a nice conversation."

Then he had to clarify how Hannah wasn't married or even involved with the father of her baby. That she was a *landscape architect.* How they had had a wonderful first date, really great, and when she gave birth a few days later he certainly wasn't going to drop her like a hot potato.

The men shook their heads and grinned in disbelief; the women, a majority of the group, looked at Tim with a new tenderness. One caught up with him on the street afterward and quoted the lyrics from "Some Enchanted Evening"—the part about "Once you have found her, never let her go." "I was afraid to say it in front of everyone, to sound so regressive," she confided.

"I didn't let her go," Tim told her. "She broke up with me."

"How long has it been?" the woman asked.

"Two years and a couple of months."

The woman looked surprised. "I thought all of us were in our acute phase."

"I know," said Tim. "I should be over her by now."

"What are we standing out in the cold for?" the woman asked.

Lucy, he discovered over coffee, *was* in her acute phase: someone named Mitchell left her unceremoniously, which she should have been prepared for because she was *his* exit relationship after being dumped by a woman from an Orthodox Jewish family.

"Are you Jewish?" she asked.

"Timothy? *McCormick?*"

She shrugged. "You could be half-Jewish. Mitchell was."

"I'm Irish Catholic," said Tim.

"What was your old girlfriend?"

"American. Norwegian-American. Her name was Thorson."

"Wow," said Lucy. "I don't know anyone from Norway. *Fjords,* right? 'The land of the midnight sun'?"

This is when I miss her the most, Tim thought.

He knows where he went wrong: asking Hannah to marry him prematurely, too soon after Alexander's birth. "We'll see," she said at first with a mysterious smile. Tim thought she was saying, Wait until my six-week checkup, until I get the go-ahead to sleep with you. Let me say yes after we've consummated our otherwise totally fulfilling relationship.

"Timothy," she would sigh when pressed, smoothing his hair affectionately, smiling the mysterious smile of one used to getting marriage proposals. "I've got too many things on my mind right now."

"Like what?" Gary asked him later, indignant.

Dealing with the baby nurse for starters, Tim told him, an agency prima donna who didn't like Hannah's marital status. . . . A painful breast infection from the nursing. . . . Worrying about day-care for Alexander when her maternity leave was over.

"The woman needs a husband and her kid needs a father," Gary insisted. "What's she trying to prove?"

Tim, who feared the worst, said he wasn't worried and only regretted his own impatience.

"Even so, let her know you won't wait forever."

Ha, thought Tim.

A married friend announces a party for all the single people she knows. Everyone whose last name begins with *A* through *L* will bring a dessert, and those whose names begin with *M* through *Z* will bring a bottle of wine. Tim says he won't come even though he's glad he falls into the wine category, and Gary says, You will, too, and I'll see to it. Audrey, the hostess, tells Gary that he can't come, because the whole idea of her party is to create a sea of eligibility: every man and woman can start up a conversation with any other guest with full confidence that the person is (a) single, (b) a professional, (c) looking, and (d) heterosexual.

"I'd only be there to make sure Tim mingles," Gary says.

Audrey shakes her head firmly.

"How many people?" Tim asks.

"Forty or fifty. Equal numbers of guys and gals."

"You'll get twenty or twenty-five desserts," Gary points out.

"I have a freezer in the garage," says Audrey.

"How do you know so many single people?" Tim asks.

"I've accumulated them over the years—college friends, co-workers, old boyfriends, old girlfriends of Patrick's who check in every few years to see if we're still married."

"Just my type," says Tim.

"Look," says Audrey, "if only two people meet at this thing, if *one* relationship gets off the ground, it will have been worth it."

"I'll come if you let Gary come."

Gary puts his arm around Audrey's waist. "I can make some lonely girl feel good for an evening. Surely you remember."

"He's lying," Audrey tells Tim.

Of course, Tim worries to himself and aloud that Hannah will be one of the twenty-five single women invited. The prospect of such an event stimulates his imagination more than usual; as it is, he sees Hannahs and blonde babies in every supermarket and department store. He calls Audrey to ask if Hannah Thorson is on her guest list, and hangs up after he's been read the names of her twenty-three women. "Do you think this is normal?" he asks Gary, who's been watching from the couch and looking pained.

"Less and less," he answers.

Gary chooses Tim's clothes for the party, allowing the khaki pleated trousers and button-down shirt, but insisting on his own skinny black silk tie, hand-painted to resemble a piano keyboard. "It makes a statement," he announces. "It says, 'Don't be fooled by my Oxford cloth and my tan bucks. I'm an artist. I am sensitive. Come talk to me. Fuck me.'"

Tim smiles weakly.

"Attitude," says Gary. "You don't walk in there tonight with that sign around your neck announcing, 'I've been hurt. Please don't you hurt me, too.' Y'know who you meet with that baggage? The walking wounded. And the mothers—the ones who knit you afghans in masculine colors after one date."

"Who do I want to meet?" Tim asks.

At Gary's insistence, they arrive an hour late. Audrey finds their name tags among the alphabetized rows in her entryway and accepts their two bottles of champagne with a triumphant smile. "It's a big success," she announces. "I'm already planning party number two."

Inside, where living room furniture once was, couples are dancing to the Beach Boys. Gary wordlessly asks a woman to dance by shifting his elbows to the music and grinning at her.

Tim crosses the dance floor to the dining room, past a table overcrowded with chocolate things, into the kitchen. Dozens of bottles of wine are cooling in the sink; unopened bakery boxes are piled on the counters. What a way to do things, he thinks—no beer, no Coke, no chips; *one* corkscrew. Well-dressed men are lifting bottles from the ice, reading the labels, and frowning. One has edited his name tag: written "Dr." in front of Audrey's peacock-blue script. No one talking to *him*, either. Tim finds the red wine breathing next to the microwave and pours himself a glass. Now to meet a woman.

Many are surveying the dessert table. They look up and smile with varying degrees of interest. Some return to the task of moving the cake plates an inch in one direction then rotating them a few degrees for maximum effect. *Mothers*, Tim remembers. He moves toward a woman who is concentrating on a slice of mocha-looking layers.

"Good?" he asks.

She closes her eyes and smiles, transported.

"Which one is it?"

The woman points to a rolled-up log.

"Mocha?" he asks.

"Mmmm. A genoise. Mocha cream and pralines." She points the tines of her fork toward her own chest. Tim shakes his head, not understanding.

"I brought it myself," she whispers.

"So?"

"Don't you think that seems a little masturbatory?"

Tim blinks.

"Have a piece," she directs.

"I can't." He holds up the wine. "I was getting this for Audrey."

"Okay," the woman says in a flat voice. "See ya."

He crosses the living room, turning his head from side to side in an exaggerated search for their hostess. She is still at the front door, greeting latecomers and mulling over the unclaimed name tags.

"Pretend you wanted this," Tim says.

"Why?"

"I had to get away from someone."

"How very mature. . . . Who was it?"

"Someone eating her own dessert. Light brown hair, white ruffled blouse."

"Melanie. Don't you read name tags?" She darts into the living room and seizes a short, curly-haired woman by the wrist. "Here you are. Beth Grace. Now go dance and enjoy yourself."

Tim smiles apologetically at Beth Grace, and she shrugs

good-naturedly. They dance a fast dance, then a slow one. He likes the way her hair curls into shiny loops and frames her face.

Gary is not particularly nice to her on the ride home, repeating "Beth Grace" in various Southern dialects until Tim explains that "Grace" is her last name; she is not a Betty-Lou or an Amanda-Sue.

"I *thought* you were a little short for a Miss America contestant," Gary says.

"Give me a break," Beth says.

"You have to get used to his humor," Tim tells her.

"No, I don't," she answers.

They drop Gary off, Tim apologizing all around, and go to her apartment. Despite his attempts to pick up threads of their party conversation and ignite the earlier spark, Beth is solemn.

"I should have sneaked out with the champagne I brought. Audrey wouldn't mind," Tim tries.

"I have some white wine in the refrigerator," Beth says.

"What did *you* bring to Audrey's?"

"Same as everyone else—chocolate truffles."

"I think I had one of those," Tim says.

He tells her about the woman at the dining room table involved with her own dessert. Beth smiles wanly, not like before.

"I'm sorry about my roommate," he repeats.

"Does he not like your meeting women or something?"

"He wants me to. He tries to help."

"Is he gay?" she asks.

Tim nods.

"Are you gay?"

"Uh-uh," says Tim.

"Does he have someone?" Beth asks. "Besides you?"

"Not that I know of," he answers.

"Is he always this hostile to women?"

"That's what's so weird," says Tim. "He's *great* with women. He could give lessons."

"Not for my money," Beth says. She leaves the room for a minute and returns with the wine, two glasses, and a bunch of green grapes in a paper towel. She leads Tim to one corner of the living room where large upholstered pillows serve as furniture.

Once settled, Beth asks how he happened to get a gay roommate.

"We worked together. He never told me, and when I asked him to live with me because I was ending a relationship—"

"With Hannah?" Beth asks.

Tim takes a swallow of wine. "You know Hannah?" he asks as casually as he can.

"No. Just the story—madonna and child. You're Audrey's favorite tragic hero."

He sees Audrey presiding at one of her dinner parties, earnestly discussing his life as if she owned shares in it. With strangers—women there tonight who read his name tag and surely said, There he is, poor Tim McCormick. "Tragic hero?" he repeats evenly.

"Don't be mad. Audrey thinks you should be over your mourning period, that's all."

Just like that, without embarrassment or apology. Five minutes ago everything seemed possible, but now he hates Audrey and this friend of hers, this smug Beth Grace.

Tim says nothing, even when he slips the skinny black tie over his ears and drops it at Gary's feet. Gary follows him into the bathroom and directs questions to the mirror while Tim brushes his teeth.

"Nice time?" he asks.

Tim holds his hand still and stares for a few seconds.

"Are you going to see her again?" Gary persists.

Tim hunches over the sink, below view. "Doubtful," he says, spitting. Why should he have to make pleasant conversation, or even act composed in his own bathroom if he's not up to it? And he isn't. There is a large knot in his stomach. Tim breathes fast to control what feels like a sob coming on. "Please leave me alone," he says.

He undresses and falls onto his bed. In the dark, he inhales and exhales in long slow breaths. The knot begins to feel looser, less localized. He pictures it decomposing, the misery spreading systemwide.

"Incredibly uptight," Gary pronounces Beth Grace on Sunday morning. "Not to mention her lack of any sense of humor whatsoever."

"You were quite the asshole yourself," Tim says.

"My Ashley Wilkes? The woman's hypersensitive."

"Can't you just say to me, 'I'm sorry? I'm sorry, Tim, that I threw cold water on everything?' Even if you didn't like her, don't you think I can decide some things for myself?"

"She wasn't so great," Gary said.

"As if you would know."

Gary picks up a section of the Sunday paper and reads, lowering it from time to time to glare at Tim and rattle the pages pointedly. After two sections in silence, Gary asks, "How would it have been different?"

"It would've," Tim says.

"You had her to yourself the rest of the time. Couldn't you undo the alleged damage?"

"It just wasn't good."

"Are we talking sex here?"

Tim shakes his head. "Things came up. About our living together. And things she heard from Audrey."

Gary shrugs. "You're lucky it soured so fast. Sometimes these things take weeks, or years." He smiles with authority. "Don't you always defer to my judgment on women? Have I been wrong yet?"

Tim answers as if he has been waiting for the question. "You were wrong about her ever coming back," he says.

Unbelievably, Alexander answers the phone. Shouts "hello"; talks.

Tim's constricted vocal cords relax in amazement. "Alexander," he shouts back. "Is your mommy there?"

"Hello? Sorry." Hannah's voice, a little breathless, overlaps the child's answer. "He beat me to it."

"Was that Alexander?" Tim asks.

There is a pause at Hannah's end. Tim hears, hopes he hears, the suggestion of a gasp. "Timothy?" she says.

"How are you?"

"Fine." She laughs. "Old and gray."

"Me, too—old and bald."

"Hard to believe," Hannah says.

"Well, older, then."

"Are you married?" she asks easily.

Oh, sure, Tim thinks. Just the guy. "No, I'm not," he says. "How about you?"

After a pause, Hannah says, "It's a long story."

"Is that a yes or a no?"

"Married? No."

Tim makes an involuntary sound, a cluck of annoyance. Hannah's goddamn life again.

Gary offers his skinny black tie, but Tim says no. They decide on blue jeans, a white shirt open at the neck, and, in case they eat out after the zoo, Gary's herringbone jacket.

Tim sits on the couch waiting so he won't be early. Gary goes into his room and comes back with a wrapped present. "A book for the kid. From you."

"Nice touch," says Tim. "Thanks."

"You saw it and loved the illustrations, so you picked it up. No big deal."

Tim takes the book. It is wrapped in plain white paper.

Gary has spelled "Alexander" in colored letters which arch across the package in an exploding rainbow.

"Go," Gary says. He walks Tim to his car. "Don't let me find all sorts of crap in my jacket pockets, like those food pellets they sell there."

"I won't," Tim promises.

"I'll probably throw some chili together tonight. Get some work done here," Gary says lightly.

"Okay," says Tim.

"So I'll be around." He opens the driver's door and tosses their gift, the wrapped book, into the back seat. Tim gets in and places it next to him on the passenger seat, rainbow up. He checks it from time to time, turns it just so as he drives, like reliable directions to a new place.

Back to Normal

His friend Audrey calls to see how things went with Beth Grace after the party.

"I'm seeing Hannah Thorson again," Tim answers, "so I guess it's a moot question."

"When did this happen?"

"I called her Sunday."

"And?"

"We got together—took her little boy to the zoo."

"I see," Audrey says.

"He's three now. A rascal." No answer, so Tim continues, "Beth Grace was very nice. I'm sure, if things were different—"

"Yeah, I know," Audrey says.

"Thanks for inviting me."

"Put Gary on," she orders.

Tim replays yesterday's scene and smiles to himself: Alexander, many shades blonder than Hannah, is stuffed into a zoo stroller, rocking himself and eating what Tim later learns is a rice cake. Hannah wears a jacket of red wool. She spots him first.

"Timothy!" he hears. He stares for a second—a needless confirmation: no one has called him "Timothy" in two and a half years. Hannah smiles but doesn't return his arcing wave. She says, as they sit on a bench and watch Alexander stomp after pigeons, that she was going to call him, too.

"Tell me everything," Hannah says during dinner. She has chosen the Thai restaurant of their first date and arranged for Alexander to sleep at his babysitter's house.

"I live with Gary. I free-lance—do catalogues for colleges that don't have their own in-house designers. Help them with their admissions brochures and stuff."

"Anyone else would call himself a consultant," says Hannah.

Tim shrugs.

"That's a compliment." She studies his face, then asks if he's been unhappy.

"Sometimes," he answers.

"Are you meeting women?"

"I meet women," Tim says, measuring the effect and noticing none.

"I'd have thought someone would've grabbed you by now."

"On the rebound?"

"I'm flattered," she says.

Tim stares: years of pain reduced to her feeling flattered. Another man might rise slowly and walk away with dignity; a James Cagney might grind a grapefruit half into Hannah's lovely cheekbones. He says, "Don't be."

She pokes one of the dishes with a serving spoon. "How many shrimp did you eat?"

"I have no idea."

"There's three left," says Hannah, "and I only want one."

Tim holds up his plate obediently as she divides and serves the seconds. "Why do you think someone would've grabbed me by now?" he asks.

Hannah chews thoughtfully. "You're the marrying type."

"That's what Gary says."

"It's true. You're nice. No one's nice anymore, especially when you get to know them."

"Women don't go for nice," Tim says.

Hannah puts out an index finger to contradict him while she chews her shrimp. She takes a sip from her water glass and announces, "Nice is coming back."

She's not talking about us, Tim realizes. She's picked me out for an eligible girlfriend and will hand me over never knowing the hopes I had for this reunion. Then she'll suggest we double-date—the girlfriend and me; Hannah and the guy she's probably living with. I'll tell Gary that you can't go home again. I'll call up Beth Grace and marry her.

"What exactly are you telling me?" he asks.

Hannah looks startled, as if her intentions are too clear to require clarification. "I'd like things to work out," she states matter-of-factly.

The complication: a boyfriend named Richard who, inconveniently enough, lived with Hannah at some critical stage in the baby's development. Alexander calls the man "Daddy." Richard loves to spend time with Alexander and has bought a family membership to the Children's Museum. There is nothing between Hannah and Richard, she explains, except the kind of bond divorced parents share when they are crazy about the same child.

"He even has a serious girlfriend now," Hannah assures Tim. Tim is skeptical. He is sure Richard brings along a casual friend to pose as a lover so Hannah will be jealous.

"Richard's still in love with you," Tim tells her. "I know the routine."

"He's honestly not. If he's in love with anything it's with Alex calling him 'Daddy.'"

"Does Alexander think the guy's his father?"

"I tell him the truth," says Hannah. "Who knows what sinks in."

"You say, 'I got pregnant on a business trip to Toronto'?"

"I say, 'Mommy wanted a little boy very much, so even though she didn't have a regular daddy living right in the house, blah blah blah . . .'"

Tim closes his eyes and shakes his head wearily.

"What am I supposed to tell him? That Daddy died in the war? Put a picture of some guy in uniform on the mantel?"

"It's not that," says Tim.

"Are you still worried about Alexander's father? Because if you are, it's like worrying about someone who donated to a sperm bank."

"I'd like a less crowded field," says Tim.

"You shouldn't be upset about Richard. It was bad timing, that's all. Babies say 'Da-Da' first, and Richard took it to heart."

Tim is not cheered. But for Hannah's breaking up with me, he figures, I'd be Da-Da, and there'd be no interloper showing up for Sunday outings.

"Was it presumptuous of me to announce I made a mistake?" Hannah asks, rather sweetly for her.

Tim clutches the hand offered him across the table as if the newly implied possibilities will be revoked.

She has bought her own house, a surprisingly boring six-room Cape in Newton. "Fenced-in yard," she explains. "Family room off the kitchen."

"It's cute," says Tim. "Cozy."

Mid-tour, Hannah stops at the refrigerator. She opens it and produces a bottle of champagne. "Do you believe my arrogance?" she says. "The cheek of a woman who would put champagne on ice before a reunion with her old boyfriend?" Hannah uncorks the champagne and pours a taste for each. She raises hers and squints with the concentration of composing a toast. "At least I didn't do *this* in advance," she says and laughs.

"To the Registry of Motor Vehicles," Tim supplies.

"Hear, hear," says Hannah.

Soon she asks, "Would it be rushing things for you and me to make love tonight?"

Gary advises caution. Hannah's return seems to him suspiciously absolute. "I need reasons," he demands.

"I didn't ask for reasons," Tim says.

"What guarantees can she give? Or are you just gonna play along until her next major decision—capital M, capital D—comes up?"

"I think she knows what she wants," Tim says quietly.

"I want to talk to her," Gary says.

Tim babysits for Alexander while Hannah meets Gary for dinner.

"I knew you when you were a baby," Tim tells him, "a tiny new baby with no hair and no teeth."

"Watch my tape," Alexander answers, unhappy whenever Tim takes his eyes off the TV screen. This is pretty easy, he thinks. Wonder if Hannah wants more—wants to have a child with him. Theirs would be blonde, too. And he wouldn't love Alexander any less.

He tries to remember being three years old, and sorts out the images which come to mind: a baby sister appearing in one of those bassinets with a skirt. No, he was almost five when Darlene was born. His grandfather's wake? Five again. First day of kindergarten? Four and a half. *Good.* Kids' memories must not go back to three. Alexander would grow up remembering no other daddy. Alexander Thorson McCormick. Alex McCormick. A damn nice guy.

Hannah tells Tim that Gary has several areas of concern: her sincerity; her capacity for long-term commitment; her flip-flopping.

"Were you able to reassure him?" he asks.

"I tried," says Hannah.

"What did you say, exactly?"

"I said there were no guarantees in this world, but, as much as any one person can go out on a limb, I was reasonably certain that I wouldn't hurt you again."

"Did that satisfy him?" Tim asks.

"He asked if I would swear on my son's life not to back down on any promises I make. So I said 'Yes.' He was extremely paternalistic, I thought, and self-righteous."

"He can be," Tim agrees.

"I mean, that kind of thing can be very sweet in a father cross-examining a man who's just asked for his daughter's hand—"

"But not from someone's gay roommate?"

Hannah nods reluctantly.

"He's still angry with you from two and a half years ago," Tim explains. "He more or less had to pick up the pieces."

"Who's Beth Grace?" asks Hannah after a few moments.

Tim has to think. Audrey's Beth Grace. "A girl I met."

"Gary said she's a fine person—emphasis on the 'fine person,' implying that she is and I'm not. Apparently she's waiting in the wings."

Beth Grace? Two dances; one glass of wine; one lousy conversation. "It hasn't been good for a long time," he tells Hannah.

Gary says he doesn't have to apologize to anyone. Later, as Tim is falling asleep, Gary proclaims through the wall that even if no one else in the apartment is interested, he'd like to hear Hannah use the word "love."

"Could she possibly have looked you up because she's pregnant again?" Tim's mother asks him.

"First of all, I called *her*. And second of all, I happen to know she has her period this week."

Mrs. McCormick winces.

"Nobody gives me much credit for having half a brain in this situation."

"Timmy," his mother says, "you fell in love with the girl when she was practically on her way to the delivery room. It's conceivable that such a thing could repeat itself and you would not go out of your way to let her pay the fiddler."

"You'd feel different if you'd met her. And Alex."

"Not the baby," his mother says. "Not until I know for sure. And if you were smart, you'd go easy, too."

"He's very well adjusted," Tim says. "He takes Hannah's relationships pretty much in stride."

Mrs. McCormick purses her lips and stares. "That's what I mean—all these relationships. Where do you come in?"

Tim shakes his head. "It's not that complicated. There's Alexander's father—totally out of the picture; and one guy Hannah dated for a while after we broke up, the one who visits Alexander. That's what? Two boyfriends in three years?"

"She broke up with you once," says Mrs. McCormick. "She runs hot and cold."

"She never made me any promises last time. Just the opposite. She was very evasive about where things stood."

"And this time?" asks his mother.

Tim grins. "We're getting married," he announces.

They tell Gary together, in a restaurant. Tim has thought, but not said, He's so civilized; he'd never make a scene at our engagement dinner.

"I'm pretty sure he's still on the side of Beth Grace," Hannah says as they wait at their table. Tim shrugs what he hopes is the shrug of a seasoned heartbreaker.

"I suppose you wonder why we've called you here tonight," Hannah intones in a baritone voice as soon as Gary appears and takes his seat.

"Let me take a wild guess."

"We're getting married," Tim says proudly.

"And Timothy in his quaint way wants your blessing," Hannah adds.

Gary rises and solemnly shakes Tim's hand. He executes an efficient quarter-turn and kisses Hannah's.

Tim exhales with relief. Gary sits down. "You weren't worried, were you?"

"Well, we knew you had certain . . . questions."

Gary dismisses his friend's statement with an impatient flick of his wrist.

"You don't?" Tim asks.

"I've made peace with the idea."

"Gee, thanks," says Hannah.

"What do you mean?" Tim asks.

"It's been pointed out to me that I'm hardly in a position to live your life for you—project my values onto you and all that."

"That's sensible," Hannah says.

"Infallible judge of character though I may be." He smiles sweetly. "So the next step was to put it in a context I could accept."

"Which is . . . ?" Tim prompts.

"A marriage for the Eighties," Gary says. "Not boy meets girl, falls in love, ditto for her, gets married . . . but its own equation. That's my new philosophy, a variation on 'live and let live.'"

Hannah raises her eyebrows. "Profound."

Gary arches his in return. "It makes for blessings, my dear, *n'est-ce pas*?"

Tim meets Hannah at her office for lunch, wearing a tie and jacket and carrying his portfolio for professional effect. The receptionist buzzes Hannah and says, without being told, "Tim's here."

"Point him in the right direction," Hannah answers through the intercom. He walks down a single carpeted hallway, bright white and skylit, to where Hannah waits in her doorway. She is wearing a dress of navy blue wool with white at the collar and cuffs, and looks wonderful, he thinks. "Do you want to see where I work?" she asks.

There is no desk, just a drafting table, the least cluttered one he's ever seen. A white parsons table against one wall holds just a telephone, an appointment book, and a message pad. "It looks like the cleaning lady just left," says Tim.

"Norwegians are neat," Hannah says. "Think of how we line those sardines up in their cans."

Then he spots the picture. It is a snapshot of Hannah holding the newborn Alexander in her hospital room, not the exact one she reproduced in quantity for birth anouncements, but one that must have followed on the roll. He is in it, sitting on the edge of Hannah's bed, drawing the baby's flannel bunting away from his pink face for better exposure.

"What's this?" he asks.

"Us," says Hannah. "Remember?"

He does. An unsuspecting nurse had taken the camera from Tim, insisting all three be in the picture. He's never seen it before, and it gives him a view of the past that he doesn't have stored in his memory.

"You didn't just put this out because I was coming here, did you?" Tim asks.

"Hardly."

"It's been here since it was taken?"

"I love it," Hannah says.

He takes it off the shelf for closer inspection, and understands why: Hannah looks happy and beautiful; Alexander, never cuter. And me, Tim thinks—for all the world a husband and a father.

"People must think it's a family portrait," he says.

Hannah takes it from Tim and wipes some invisible dust away with her fingertips. She smiles at it, and puts it back on the shelf.

"Was it here all along?"

Hannah nods.

"In this incredibly neat office where it seems highly unlikely you'd have an outdated photograph of someone you broke up with years before, collecting dust?"

"What's the matter?" Hannah asks.

"I'm thinking, Maybe it's for the clients—the office equivalent of your soldier on the mantel. Why else would you keep a picture of me around? Didn't your other boyfriends visit your office and wonder who the guy is sitting on your bed, holding your baby?"

Hannah closes the door to her office. "Why are you getting so agitated about a picture?"

Tim paces back and forth a few times, jangling the contents of his pockets. "I don't know," he repeats every turn. "I don't know." He picks up the picture again. "Maybe I fill the bill: husband, father, *nice.* The right guy at the right time. Maybe that's why you're marrying me—we make a nice family portrait."

Hannah takes the photo back and puts it face down by the telephone. "You know what I think?" she asks. "I think you were angry with me for two and a half years, and there hasn't been any reason to pick a fight since we're back together. But now it's safe: we're getting married. So you've picked some weird little thing to fixate on."

Tim thinks about Hannah's analysis, recognizes its merit but doesn't want to acknowledge how uncomplicated his anger is. "Maybe we shouldn't have lunch today," he says.

Hannnah doesn't react at first, then makes a great show of pulling an extremely stubborn, invisible ring off her finger. "Do you want it back?" she asks. "Just say the word." She tugs some more, uses her knees for leverage — a burlesque of ring removal. "I suppose I could wear it on a chain around my neck, and we could just go steady while you're deciding," she says with a sigh.

He is tempted to smile and have it done with, even to come back with a high school joke about letting him go all the way now that she's his steady. But he doesn't. "When you broke up with me, you said you couldn't ever love me the way I loved you," he says, "so maybe this is the appropriate time to ask if that's still true."

Hannah stares straight ahead into his chin for a moment. Finally she says firmly, "I wouldn't marry you if that were still true." She moves a step closer, kisses him, smiles to prompt his smile. Tim stares back at beautiful Hannah, considers this answer and, sadly, other words she might have used.

Memorial Day

Tim drives, and Hannah teases him by coaching Alexander for most of the fifteen-minute ride from Cambridge to Arlington. "Say, 'How do you do, Step-Grandmama?'"

Alexander catches on that a joke is in the making. "Stepma," he shouts from the back seat. "Stepma stepma stepma."

"That's perfect," Hannah tells her son. "And be sure to give her lots of kisses." She leans sideways as far as her seat belt allows to nudge Tim with her elbow.

Tim waits for what he hopes is a nonchalant interval before asking, "He won't really call her that, will he?"

"We'll see," says Hannah airily.

"Not that she won't love him at first sight."

"That would be nice," says Hannah.

"And you, too," Tim adds.

"You McCormicks," says Hannah. "An impetuous lot."

Tim thinks for a minute. "In our own fashion," he says.

Hannah pats his knee. "And three years later, we're off to meet Mother."

"Muvver," Alexander repeats from the back seat.

"Mine," says Tim. "Tim's mother." He checks the little boy's face in the rearview mirror. Alexander is staring out the window, smiling, as if Tim's having a mother is grounds for another joke.

"Mrs. McCormick," Hannah says. "We're going to Mrs. McCormick's house for dinner—the house Tim lived in when he was a little boy."

"I know that," says Alexander.

"And," Hannah says in a sing-song undertone that only Tim can hear, "if she can deal with her son getting engaged to a fallen woman, she can become your grandmother."

"C'mon," says Tim.

"Don't worry. I will be perfectly gracious. We'll all be perfectly gracious."

"She's a nice lady. From the old school, but a nice lady."

"So am I," says Hannah.

It is the cocktail hour in Edina, Minnesota. Hannah's parents drink a split of champagne and discuss the wedding.

"We'll make a vacation of it," says Mr. Thorson. "Stay in Boston a few days, then fly down to Bermuda. Or maybe spend the rest of the week in New York and use the firm's apartment."

"Boston?" says Mrs. Thorson. "I can't imagine they're thinking of getting married in Boston."

"They're all there," he reminds her. "His family, too."

"Do you know for sure? Did they specifically say *not* Minneapolis?"

Mr. Thorson holds both palms up to fend off her interrogation. "When my daughter calls to announce she's getting married—at age thirty-four, thank you very much—I don't argue the fine points. I say, God's in His heaven, all's right with the world."

Mrs. Thorson smiles. "I know. Aren't we absolutely *parental* about the whole thing: he walks, he talks, he's white. We approve."

"A slight exaggeration. I like to think I have a nose for a solid son-in-law."

"I know she loves him," his wife adds.

Mr. Thorson lifts his glass. "Here's to whatever it took: Love. Sense. A kick in the derrière."

Mrs. Thorson clinks her glass with his, but doesn't drink. "I'd love to have it here," she muses. "I've always pictured Hannah walking down the front stairway . . . white jonquils lining the foyer."

Her husband shrugs. "Ask her. All she can do is refuse." Mrs. Thorson arches her eyebrows.

He corrects himself: "All she can do is make you sorry you ever asked." They smile indulgently, grateful for the problems a daughter's wedding entails.

Tim and Hannah arrange themselves at his mother's front door. Alexander sits on Tim's shoulders; Hannah holds a flowering plant, and smiles in readiness for the door opening. The little boy insists he press the doorbell with his toe. Tim crouches to let him, and the door opens immediately. Mrs. McCormick gasps with admiration.

"This can't be Alexander," she says in a voice filled with theatrical wonder. "I heard he was just a little boy. You're taller than Timmy!"

Alexander shrieks with delight. "I sitting on him!" he yells.

Mrs. McCormick slaps her cheek. "Silly me. I thought you were so tall that you wouldn't fit through my doorway!"

Tim pulls Alexander up over his head and down to the ground in one graceful swoop.

"See!" the little boy shouts. "See!"

Mrs. McCormick puts out her hand and Alexander takes it. Like the closing frames of a Shirley Temple movie, adult and child march happily across the threshold. Hannah, hanging back a few seconds, blinks her eyes comically at Tim as if she's witnessed something otherworldly.

Hannah's parents call their housekeeper into the dining room to mediate. "Tell me what your rules are about getting married," Mrs. Thorson commands. "Donald says Catholics have rules."

Fanny puts the dish towel over her shoulder and sits down. "You have to be married by a priest. Second, it has to be in a Catholic church unless you get special permission—"

"What about the contract you sign that promises you'll raise your children Catholic?" Mr. Thorson asks impatiently.

"That's true. If one of them's not Catholic. Then there's the pre-Cana conferences. They come first. Then posting the marriage banns. It depends on the priest and also the parish. Some are more modern than others. You can usually find a Jesuit who's less a stickler on the laws."

Mrs. Thorson shakes her head as if it's all too ridiculous to pursue. "There must be easier ways for a Catholic to intermarry. I guarantee Hannah's not signing any religious documents."

"It's not binding in any court," says her husband. "It's more or less a courtesy to the host church, I would imagine."

"Timothy might be counting on a wedding Mass," says Fanny. "You don't know how religious his people are."

"We don't know the slightest thing about his people," Mrs. Thorson tells Fanny. "Hannah says the mother is widowed. I don't dare ask what his father did."

"That's what our daughter would consider an elitist question," her husband explains with a mocking smile. "And we're avoiding all controversy until June first."

"That's the date?" Fanny asks.

"They said 'early spring.' Donald and I are going to push for Memorial Day weekend so some of the flowering trees will be in bloom." Mrs. Thorson turns to the windows which face the garden, and squints into the dark.

"Hannah says they'll definitely have it in Edina?" the housekeeper asks.

Mrs. Thorson doesn't answer. Her husband and Fanny have already receded; the dining room furniture has been replaced with folding chairs, and she imagines the Reverend Gronseth, *their* Reverend Gronseth, standing here—no *there*, with the forsythias as a backdrop—looking particularly distinguished in his wedding-white robes.

After dinner, Tim takes Alexander up to the attic where Mrs. McCormick remembers having last seen her son's old toys. It is not a graceful exit, Hannah thinks; every feature on Tim's face was signaling, "Time for the women to talk alone."

Hannah is about to launch into compliments on the meal, and on Mrs. McCormick's way with Alexander, but Tim's mother speaks first.

"He's crazy about you," she says quietly.

"I know," Hannah says after a pause.

"He's never wanted to marry anyone else before."

"Neither have I."

"Never?" asks Mrs. McCormick.

Hannah thinks for a few moments. "I was always in love with someone in high school. And of course I was going to marry every one of those. I probably have the doodles in my notebooks to prove it."

"I guess I meant the father," Tim's mother says. "Timmy doesn't say much on the subject."

Hannah is about to say, "I got pregnant on a business trip

to Toronto. The man never called. I decided to have the baby"—the shortened version of the much-requested explanation. Instead, she asks, "What can I say that will reassure you?"

"I'm not sure," Mrs. McCormick says.

"You're worried that Alexander's father is a factor?"

"I suppose I am," she says.

"He's not," says Hannah.

Mrs. McCormick puts her hands flat on the table, palms down, and stares at them. Hannah notices that her fingernails shine with a pinky-clear lacquer she hasn't seen on anyone since her grandmother died. "He's such a sweet boy," the older woman says, as if noting the irony of his undeserved misfortune.

"Timothy?" asks Hannah.

"He's never been one to chase girls for the fun of it. Even when he was younger, fifteen and sixteen, he'd get a crush on some girl in study hall and take the whole year to ask her out. His friends would come over and sit on the porch and talk about girls—a lot of bragging and fresh talk. But not Timmy. It never came easy to him. And he was the nicest looking of the lot."

She wants a declaration in shorthand, Hannah thinks: Isn't Timmy sweet? Good-looking? True blue? *Reassure me that you love him as much as such sweetness and goodness deserve. Tell me before they come back downstairs; before I buy a dress for the wedding.*

"Do you have any pictures of Timothy from high school?" Hannah asks.

Mrs. McCormick looks surprised, but pleased. She leaves

the room and returns in seconds with a huge graduation portrait. Hannah recognizes it as the top of any portrait studio's line: color applied by oil onto the sepia yearbook pose. His hazel eyes have been painted a clear green, and his brown hair is highlighted with gold brush strokes—a chromatically idealized Tim. "His face has filled out," says his mother.

"What a cutie," says Hannah, taking the portrait from Mrs. McCormick and propping it on her lap. "I think I would have had a crush on him."

"*Would* of?" the older woman asks.

"If I had known him in high school. I went for those skinny track-team types."

Tim's mother walks around the table and sits down in her chair. "I guess you didn't have any trouble getting boys," she says to Hannah.

Don't have trouble getting boys. This is what a snide mother of an unpopular girl says to the mother of a popular one, Hannah reasons. It is also applicable to a future daughter-in-law with an illegitimate child by another man.

But what is the goal here? Hannah reminds herself. "Did I say something wrong, Mrs. McCormick?" she asks.

"No," the older woman answers too quickly.

"Have I been talking too much about old high school heartthrobs?"

"Not that," says Tim's mother.

"Something about Timothy?"

Mrs. McCormick nods.

"Don't worry," says Hannah. "Just say it."

"You're very . . . casual the way you talk about him. I think that's the word I would use."

"Could you give me an example?" Hannah asks.

Mrs. McCormick stares at the wall just above Hannah's head. After a long pause she says, "It's just a feeling I get."

Hannah smiles reassuringly. "That's just me. I don't declare my feelings from the rooftops. I'm very Scandinavian in that way."

"This is not a rooftop," says Mrs. McCormick carefully. "I am the boy's mother."

Hannah nods slowly. "I really love your son a lot," she says.

The Thorsons reach Hannah at home after dinner. "Darling," her mother says, "let's pin down a date and a place. I have to get started."

Hannah motions for Tim to run upstairs and pick up the extension. "Timothy's getting on," she says. "One second." They are silent until they hear his click.

"Mother wants us to decide where to get married."

"Good," says Tim.

"The choices as I see them are here at home, or there," says Mrs. Thorson.

Hannah laughs. "'Here at home in your beautiful birthplace, or there in a sterile restaurant, far from your loved ones.'"

"Don't put words in my mouth. . . . Does she do that to you, too, Timothy?"

"She likes to pull my leg."

"Have you thought about it?" Hannah's mother persists.

"Logistically, it makes sense to have it in Massachusetts,"

says Hannah. "There's fewer of you to fly here than vice versa."

"That's true." Mrs. Thorson pauses. Hannah prays her mother won't offer to pay for Tim's family's tickets. "But should *convenience* be our sole criterion?" she asks.

"What would you and Mr. Thorson like?" asks Tim.

"Something simple right here in the house. Ceremony in the dining room overlooking the garden. Reception outside, weather permitting."

"When?" Hannah asks her mother.

"We see May thirtieth as the earliest possible date."

Hannah sighs. "It seems inefficient to bring everyone out to Minnesota, when we probably should just cab everyone over to Cambridge City Hall."

"That is certainly true," says Mrs. Thorson, "but this way, *we* handle all the details and it's more like a holiday for everyone. People don't mind traveling for weddings. And, of course, they'll be our guests at whatever hotel you decide."

"I don't know," says Hannah. "Why don't we discuss it and call you back."

"Don't forget that Fanny will be here to take care of the baby. And you can leave him here when you honeymoon," her mother adds to sweeten the offer.

"That's very tempting," says her daughter.

"What about your family, Tim?" asks Mrs. Thorson, magnanimous so close to victory. "Would they like to spend a few days in Edina?" *See the nice family I come from, Mrs. McCormick,* Hannah thinks. *Such a nice house and a nice town for an unwed mother to grow up in. Surprised?* There is no response from Tim, so Hannah's mother points out that it *is* a first marriage for them both and they are *entitled* to all festivities. When he doesn't answer, Hannah prompts, "What'll it be? Your place or mine?"

"Oh, what the hell," he says happily.

Tim explores the Thorsons' second floor and counts bedrooms: his, Hannah's, Alexander's (Hannah's nursery, decorated during her ballerina phase); Fanny's, now unused because she works days and no longer lives in; and the big suite that is the Thorsons'. Tim doesn't walk across their threshold to see the sauna or the tiled, walk-in bath with six shower heads Hannah has told him about. He carries his new bathrobe and shaving kit, and stops every few yards as if lost. If someone finds him wandering upstairs, he'll merely ask which of the guest bathrooms he's been assigned. Hannah and Alexander are napping. The dinner guests arrive at eight.

He and Hannah joked beforehand about sleeping arrangements. Tim was sure the Thorsons would assign separate bedrooms. Hannah thought her parents would double them up, wanting to express their approval of Tim, and their liberal-mindedness. When they arrived and were shown to their separate and distant rooms, Mrs. Thorson apologized: Fanny, after all, would be making—and in her Old-World way, counting—the beds that Hannah and her fiancé slept in.

It is Fanny who finds him now exploring the second floor.

"Good thing you came along," he says. "I didn't want to wake Hannah just to ask which bathroom was mine."

"The green one, next to the nursery," says Fanny.

"Thank you," says Tim.

Fanny does not keep walking. "When does your mother arrive?" she asks.

"Tomorrow."

Fanny smiles conspiratorially. "My maiden name was O'Donnell," she tells him. Catholics, her fraternal look suggests; the servant and the widowed mother-in-law. Tim has cousins named O'Donnell, but he decides not to tell Fanny.

"Thanks for the directions," he says and takes a few steps toward the green bathroom.

"Where'd you go to college?" Fanny asks.

"U.Mass," Tim tells her.

"Never heard of it."

"The University of Massachusetts."

"Is that near Mount Holyoke College?" asks Fanny.

"Pretty near," says Tim.

"That's where Hannah went. It's for very smart girls."

"I know," says Tim.

"But you didn't know her then?"

Tim nods.

"Not until she was already pregnant, if I got it right."

"She was in front of me in line at the Registry of Motor Vehicles. I couldn't see her stomach," he recites in a flat voice.

Fanny nods as if it's all coming back to her. "That's one for the books, all right."

Soon, Tim thinks—tomorrow—it'll be "groom" or "husband," or "stepfather," instead of Tim the curiosity, the only guy in history who fell in love with a woman in her last trimester. Soon.

Judge Baskin turns out to be younger than they had guessed from phone conversations—fortyish—with rusty hair and a plump, freckled face. He wins everyone over during rehearsal by singing tomorrow's music in what sounds like an arrangement for a high school marching band. Dinner is served afterward to members of the wedding and to a dozen of the Thorsons' best friends who haven't met Tim. Mr. Thorson produces a bottle of champagne with a tiny ballerina inside which he received when Hannah was born, and had saved for her wedding.

"It's aged a bit longer than I'd originally intended," he says with a wry smile as he toasts the couple. Following their host's lead, other guests toast Hannah and Tim, and find clever ways to footnote the story of their courtship. Paul and Dana from Hannah's firm perform a skit they confess to have rehearsed on company time: of Hannah, very pregnant, applying to an executives-only dating service. The three parents watch with sour half-smiles.

Tim's roommate and best man, Gary, stands and says, "Let's call a spade a spade. My buddy here owes it all to that pregnant belly." He puts an arm around Tim's shoulder and jerks him close. "Remember, this is not a guy who automatically makes a move on a beautiful blonde and comes away with a phone number. I know. I was there from Day One. He thought he was shooting the breeze with a nice, unavailable lady who had the good sense to call him up and lay her cards on the table. That fat belly gave him confidence." Gary raises his glass. "To Alexander," he says, winking at Hannah. Hannah stands up. She walks around the table and kisses Gary. The parents hold their half-smiles, while everyone else blinks back tears. Judge Baskin predicts a great time tomorrow.

When he's sure the Thorsons are asleep and Fanny has gone home, Tim visits Hannah's room and finds her awake. "Everyone had a good time, I think," he tells her.

"Even you?"

He smiles. "I had the same conversation with every person there. I could have had a note pinned to my jacket with the answers: 'Graphic designer.' 'Arlington, Massachusetts.' 'No, she was already pregnant when I met her.'"

Hannah laughs. "No one actually asked you outright, did they?"

Tim shakes his head.

"Not in this crowd," she adds.

"What *do* they know?" asks Tim.

"My mother's version: modern daughter produces grandchild during coffee break at high-power job. Something like that. No nod to there being sperm involved. She tells it as if she's bragging. . . . No one suspects she almost cracked up over it."

"My mother would've gone straight to the crack-up and skipped the part about making it glamorous," says Tim.

"*Your* mother wouldn't have called me every day for three months begging me to have an abortion."

"True," says Tim.

Hannah gives one of her pillows to Tim. "Get in," she instructs, holding the covers up tent-like. "I don't want to sleep alone on my pre-wedding night."

Tim gingerly removes his shoes and unzips his trousers. "Isn't it bad luck or something? Especially in your parents' house?"

"Foolish superstition," says Hannah.

Grinning, Tim pulls off his underwear and sends it over his shoulder with a swashbuckling toss. "Guess I'm just an old-fashioned guy," he says. He gets into bed, sliding his arm under Hannah's neck and bringing her body to rest against his. Hannah finds his wrist and checks the luminescent dial of his watch.

"Almost two," says Hannah. "Ten more hours."

Tim exhales slowly.

"Are you nervous about tomorrow?" she asks.

"Are you?"

"No. But then again I'm not a carefree man-about-town settling down to dream my last dreams of bachelorhood," Hannah points out.

Tim turns to her, kisses her bare shoulder, her mouth; thinks to himself, then says, "Neither am I."

Gary videotapes the wedding, his gift to Hannah and Tim. They watch the uncut version on the Thorsons' king-sized bed before leaving for the airport. It opens with Gary clumsily focusing on a newspaper dateline in his hotel room. "Today is the wedding of my best friend, Tim McCormick, to Hannah Thorson. It is sunny in downtown Minneapolis, approximately sixty-two degrees Fahrenheit," Gary narrates. "Now I'll be heading over to the Thorsons' place in Edina to see how things are going."

Dark pink rhododendron blossoms come into focus next. Gary has set the camera up on the front lawn to interview whoever comes along. "What makes this wedding special from others you've done?" he asks the florist.

"No one ever interviewed me before," he answers, squinting with the effort.

"Do you have any cooking tips for the bride?" he asks the caterers, two sisters with the same curly black hair and rimless glasses.

"Why don't you ask that again without the male bias?" one answers.

"Get a microwave," says the other.

Hannah and Tim are treated to the history of the harpsichord by the harpsichordist, and a description by Mrs. Thorson's hairdresser of what she'll be doing to Mrs. Thorson.

They check their watches and fast-forward to the ceremony. Hannah stops when she comes to a long, blank shot of the empty staircase. "Here we go," she announces. In seconds, faint, tinny chords of "Here Comes the Bride" are heard, accompanied by the louder sounds of chairs scraping and guests murmuring.

"I couldn't see this from where I was standing," Tim whispers. Hannah appears. She wears her mother's wedding dress, ivory satin with flowing sleeves, and a crown of baby's breath on her blonde hair. She walks down the stairs regally, her back straight, her ivory kid shoes peeking out from the hem of her dress with each confident step.

"You look so beautiful," Tim says.

Hannah nods once, intent on the images. Mr. Thorson waits at the bottom of the flight, watching his daughter's descent. The angle is wrong and they can't see his face. "He was smiling," Hannah tells Tim. "Grinning, actually. That's what made me smile . . . *there.*"

Tim leans forward and touches the TV screen. "This is where you came into view—when the guests straightened up and faced forward again. As soon as I saw you smiling, I relaxed. Sort of."

"You look great," says Hannah. "Very distinguished."

"I thought my pants were too short."

Hannah freezes the action with the remote control. "Maybe a hair," she says after a few moments of study.

The ceremony begins. The camera has been fixed on a tripod to one side of Judge Baskin so that Gary may perform his best-man duties. The faces of Hannah and Tim fill the screen.

"The miracle of video," says Hannah. "I was staring into Baskin's vest for practically the whole ceremony, yet now I'm able to watch both of us for every second. It's like *Our Town,* where the dead people sit on ladders and watch the stories of their lives."

"Romantic," says Tim.

They watch in silence and listen to their voices repeat the civil vows. "Nice," Hannah says. "Right to the point."

Tim nods in agreement without taking his eyes off the screen. After a few moments he says, "My voice sounded shaky. Could you tell?"

Hannah smiles. "It was nice." Sounding weaker than the assured tones coming from the tape she adds, "Tender." She stares straight ahead. Tim sees tears forming in her eyes.

"Are you crying?" he asks. She shakes her head.

"Are you upset?"

When she doesn't answer Tim thinks, Now I know. She's watching us get married and she's helpless. She can't rewind the tape and call it off. She's sorry she ever did it. Hannah who never cries is crying. He reaches for the control and stops the tape.

"Timothy," she says with some exasperation. "I'm watching my own wedding and it's very moving. Would you stop worrying. Please."

Tim presses "play," but turns to her every few seconds under the guise of sharing videotaped moments. She presses the corners of her eyes with the knuckle of her index finger.

Then Hannah and Tim on tape are pronounced husband and wife. They kiss with their eyes open and with slightly foolish smiles, as if they're too old and sensible to play bride and groom in costume.

Hannah, watching on the big bed, sighs and rests her head on Tim's shoulder for a moment. When her eyes return to the screen, he rubs his shoulder against his cheek to feel the damp circle her tears have left. Wonderful tears, he decides; *tears.*

In years to come, the actual wedding and the viewing of the tape merge into one ceremony, one edited memory. Tim will think that the camera's sighting Hannah at the top of the stairs was his own perspective and that the harpsichord, like his own voice, was barely audible.

He will splice her tears into his private version of their wedding, and swear against the evidence that Hannah Thorson cried with happiness as she became his wife.

You're Right, I Know You're Right

When I meet Claire in the market and ask her a question about herself, she thanks me for being such a good friend, and is likely to send a small gift. A cup of coffee in my kitchen produces a thank-you note from her in the next day's mail. She apologizes for coming empty-handed when she stops by to retrieve a book I borrowed and failed to return. She tries so hard to please and to be liked that she appears frantic most of the time. I have left her apartment with a public television program guide or an unopened roll of paper towels as a parting gift because I refused to take the leftovers from dinner or the flowers she arranged for the table.

Claire works, and has always worked, for nonprofit agencies that pay her low-to-moderate wages. Her nervous energy translates well into job performance, where her perfect manners and graciousness come across as confident charm. She has worked for charities, hospitals, museums, foundations, and universities in the fourteen years since we graduated from the same women's college, changing positions for a genteel salary increase or the illusion of nicer colleagues. My theory about her job history is that she has an unconscious wish to be a volunteer for the same charitable organizations that employ her. She was brought up to be the mistress of a home, the wife of a successful man who commutes by train into the city and whose tax bracket prohibits his wife from doing anything for a salary.

Claire grew up in a Massachusetts mill town—a wealthy Protestant in a city of ethnic, working-class Catholics. Her mother called Claire's father "Doctor" when speaking about him to patients or friends: "Doctor likes his dinner at six," she would say. Or "Doctor has rounds at the hospital this morning."

Claire was their fourth daughter and next-to-last try before producing a son who is now his father's partner. Claire apologizes for the size of her family. She feels, apparently, that her failure to be born male caused her parents to have an undignified, practically Catholic number of children. And she was named for her mother, as if all the favored girls' names were exhausted after three, and one already circulating in the large white house would do as a thrifty choice.

Claire insists that Deirdre, the oldest, is the family beauty, and that Martha, Gwendolyn, and Charles Junior were exceptional scholars and athletes. Her parents never bestowed any titles on Young Claire, as they call her—not easiest baby, or kindest or healthiest or most artistic child—just last daughter, the unmarried one, who lives away from home.

I run into Claire every few weeks. We do our Saturday errands in the same village center and she always insists on treating me to coffee. She has generally met a new man between these meetings of ours. She meets a lot of men. They are attracted to her from the other sides of airport terminals and at the national conferences she attends for her nonprofit agency employers. She is a little taller than average, about five-foot-six, with dark hair perfectly cut into thick bangs above gray-blue eyes and sleek straight sides that curve under slightly at her collar. She is always perfectly groomed, dressed in sundresses of expensive dark cotton in the summer and outfits of pastel wool crepe in the winter.

Except for Phil, none of the men Claire has gotten involved with since we've been having coffee has lasted more than a few months. In every case the man has backed away first. Only one said why—that she made him nervous. The others just stopped calling. Claire would let a week pass, then write the man a note enclosing a newspaper clipping. They were always cut from *The New York Times* and were always a feature about a topic the man had mentioned in conversation: passive solar heat, making wine at home, Shaker reproductions, restocking the Connecticut River with salmon. She clips articles for all her friends and leaves them in our mailboxes. I am inexplicably irritated by these clippings, the way unnecessary thank-you notes and house gifts irritate me, and I can only assume that she irritates the men she clips for as well. When someone doesn't respond to her notes, she asks me if she should call him to save this most recent lover the embarrassment of calling after not calling for so long. Sometimes she asks my permission to stage a confrontation, and I dissuade her, knowing how apologetic she will be. If she is determined to see the unresponsive suitor one last time, I suggest she surprise him.

"I can't just drop over," Claire says. "But I was thinking of calling and saying I was going to be in his neighborhood and thought I'd pick up my pie plate if it was convenient."

"Does that sound like a confrontation?" I demand. "Do you sound like a person who's been hurt?"

"No," she says meekly. "You're right. You're so good at knowing what to do. You're a wonderful friend."

"And don't bring a gift," I warn.

Claire looks troubled. "I was going to bring him some flowers and a clipping he'd like on the restoration of a Victorian beach house on Block Island."

"No flowers," I say. And more emphatically, "No clipping! Go home and rip it up."

Claire sighs. She doesn't agree. I may as well be advising her to eat dinner at a friend's house and not rise after dessert to clear the table.

"What will it say to him, your clipping? That you've been thinking about him? That despite his rotten behavior—ignoring you and not calling for weeks, then being abrupt and sarcastic when you call him—he still deserves your thoughtfulness? What kind of a message is that?"

"You're right," she says, crying a little from the cumulative pain of so many six-week romances that she didn't want to end and the inefficacy of so much niceness.

"Thank you for listening," she says. "Thank you for being such a good friend." The next day a note on pretty paper falls through my mail slot, thanking me for listening and for being such a friend.

It is a little hard on Claire that I am married and that my husband is a sweet man. If she telephones weekends or evenings, she begins and ends the conversation by saying how sorry she is to be taking me away from Neil. She is nervous in his presence and is her most frantically nice self. Her compliments pour out in run-on sentences that can't be interrupted or answered: "Nora tells me that you're both taking a week off to do *nothing,* just work around the house, which is just so perfect for you two because you're both so creative and energetic that you'll accomplish so much and enjoy each other's company and probably just cook those wonderful meals you collaborate on. . . . I cut out a recipe Sunday from the magazine section for blackened swordfish. I'll send it to you."

Neil never knows how to respond to Claire's high-speed one-way conversation. He usually smiles, excuses himself, tells me later that she drives him crazy, and asks what I see in her. It was he who pointed out that Claire has only two speeds—nice and more nice. I suspect this is absolutely true in her relationships. When things go wrong, and the men begin to pull away, Claire tries even harder with more notes, more clippings, more pies. If someone says he can't go out Friday night because he's working until five-fifteen and has to get up early Saturday to sail, Claire offers to cook his dinner. If he says he's too tired and is picking up takeout, she offers to buy the food and deliver it.

"I shouldn't have done that, should I?" she asks when she describes such invitations and sees me wince.

Claire is now having what she calls an affair. I have learned that affairs are what Claire has with unsuitable men—Catholic, Jewish, or non-Caucasian men; those who are younger than she and those who are not attorneys, doctors, architects, academics, MBAs, or executive officers of nonprofit agencies.

I am keen on Claire's current affair with Phil Casciotti, our produce man. He is bright and attentive, and makes the fruit and vegetable section the most interesting part of the market. When Claire first told me she was having dinner with him, she used the phrase "just for fun" at least six times in her explanation.

Phil told Claire that he doesn't socialize with customers, but was too drawn to her and too impressed by her unfailing courtesy not to pursue the matter. She always asked him thoughtful, earnest questions: where things were grown, which potatoes held up best in chowder, how to tell if a melon is ripe without squeezing it. She was one of the few customers who didn't sample the bing cherries and seedless grapes, and she complimented him when something she bought tasted especially good. It began when Phil weighed Claire's fruits and vegetables and marked the bag with some price well below its actual cost. After several weeks of such conspicuous favoritism, Claire told Phil she felt guilty about the markdowns. "Would it assuage your guilt to discuss it over a drink some evening?" he had asked. Admiring his charm and vocabulary, she said yes.

Claire is apologetic about Phil and tells me that she hadn't had sex in eleven months when they met and, at thirty-five, is supposed to be at the height of her sexual energy. She is strongly attracted to him, and repeats to me in a voice filled with discovery that Phil's family came from the north of Italy where people look more Bavarian than Mediterranean, accounting for his straight fair hair and almond-shaped green eyes. She also says frequently what a good person he is, a genuinely good person, with a little bafflement in her voice as if to say that men of her acquaintance don't generally come that way, and isn't it ironic that Phil, a fling, is so much nicer than the future-husband types she has met.

She is further puzzled by Phil's love of children, the way he plucks babies out of shopping carts and holds them over his head and makes them laugh and memorizes the regulars' names. None of the men she knows through work or meets through her family carry on the way Phil does when a baby passes by in a backpack or a stroller.

Phil must have sensed, after seeing Claire's heirloom Persian rugs, her collection of sugar tongs, and her pale-blue monogrammed sheets, that his credentials mattered. He feeds her details about himself which she feeds to me. He has a degree in fine arts and wants to learn the fruit and vegetable business from the ground up. He hopes to own his own market within five years, and to run a wholesale business that will supply fruits and vegetables to fine restaurants. His store will have fresh herbs year-round and possibly a cheese section.

Claire doesn't want her family to know about her affair. Her sisters are all married to what seems like the same person—a tall, athletic stockbroker with tortoiseshell glasses and a squash racket in his briefcase. She says her parents would not be pleased even with Phil's dream, and would be repelled by his current position.

I prompt Claire to see her relationship with him as something other than an affair. She calls him "my friend Phil." When I ask how things are going, she uses phrases like "We have a lot of fun together" and "It's nice to just enjoy the moment." He is younger than she, Claire reminds me, just thirty, a Catholic, and he doesn't own a suit.

Phil would like them to live together. Claire says it isn't practical because he has to be at the wholesaler's at 4 A.M. six days a week and she wouldn't be able to let him leave the house without making his breakfast. She says they have worked out a nice schedule of early dinners, early-evening lovemaking, and Saturday night sleepovers. Meanwhile, when a divorced stockbroker gets her telephone number from a brother-in-law, or when a single doctor who has attended a medical convention with her father calls for a date, she feels obliged to accept. She has to look down the road, she says, and she mustn't be rude to a friend of the family.

It is obvious that Phil is crazy about Claire, even though it has only been several months since their first drink. He grins uncontrollably when we shop together Saturday mornings, and reduces the price of my fruit, too, simply by association. The other produce people, who report to Phil, know about the romance, and run to cold storage for the freshest still-unpacked produce when Claire appears.

You're Right, I Know You're Right

Claire kept Phil a secret from her family for almost six months, until a sister dropped by unannounced one Sunday noon between church and a museum visit. Phil and Claire, who were reading the paper in bed, managed to scramble into their clothes and arrange the covers, but they couldn't dispel the air of intimacy and the look they both wore of having been recently asleep. Phil was introduced to Gwendolyn and her husband as Phil Casciotti, with no further designation. That night, Claire's mother called and wanted to know who this fellow Cacciatore was. She corrected her mother without chiding her for the corruption of his name, and said he was someone she was seeing. "What is he in?" her mother asked. "Fruits and vegetables," Claire whispered. Her mother was silent. "Commodities?" she asked hopefully. "Yes," her daughter said, lying for the first time in her adult life.

She told me this over coffee several weekends later. She looked tearful and said her parents were being quite cool with her because they have figured out she is sleeping with Phil. Getting engaged or married would not pacify them because they do not find him suitable. Gwendolyn had told them he looked quite young, quite physical, and not like a professional. Choosing Phil would mean estranging herself from her family, even though they would be polite and correct and invite them to the family celebrations of holidays and promotions. They had several nice men in mind, her age or older, whose parents they knew.

Into Love and Out Again

Claire didn't know how to break up with Phil because she had never had to end a relationship herself. She thought it would be best to cook dinner and tell him in person, and after that shop at another market for a while. They would both be miserable, but Phil was young and handsome and would find a woman to marry whose family would brag to their friends about his entrepreneurial skills. She would try to keep busy—have lunch with her sisters more often, learn to quilt, perhaps look for a new job. She would write a note to Phil's mother, whom she had never met but might have hurt, to explain things and apologize. She thought she would send a gift to the produce people to thank them for their help and courtesy, and now their understanding. And she would keep in touch with Phil—cards at his birthday and at Christmas, and a split-leaf philodendron for the opening of his store.

Obit

There was another woman's picture above my name in the morning paper, and the "Jo-Ann" was spelled without my hyphen, but I inhaled sharply just the same. "Jo Ann E. Foote," the obituary said. "Was teacher, 63." I knew I was just thirty-nine and clearly alive, eating cinnamon toast at my desk, but I touched my face to be sure. I am in my office, I thought. Here is my blotter, my calendar (I checked the date from years of watching "Twilight Zone"); my pen-and-pencil set, my telephone, my in-box, my out-box. Reassured, I waited for the phone calls and read about the other Jo Ann Foote.

She was single, too, and dead after a long illness. Survived by nieces and nephews; a graduate of Salem Normal School; spent summers in Pocasset on the Cape. A teacher with sidelines, she had started her own after-school business delivering balloon bouquets for all occasions.

My mother called first.

"I had the worst fright," she said.

"I know."

"It leaped out at me and I thought *automobile accident.*"

"They'd notify the next-of-kin first," I said.

Mother sighed. "That's still me, isn't it?"

I picked up the newspaper again and backed up one spread. I turned slowly, pretending I was an innocent reader scanning headlines. Would my friends see my name there at the top inside column? The dominant obituary, accompanied by a photograph, was that of a retired editor of the *New England Journal of Medicine*—four or five times the length of Jo Ann Foote's. Maybe some doctors I had dated would see it and call me.

I buzzed Maggie on the intercom. "Turn to page twenty-seven in the morning *Globe,*" I said and hung up. I listened for the delay that usually followed my requests, then a lackadaisical swish of pages. Finally, I heard her footsteps and she opened my office door. "How do you want me to handle this?" she asked.

"Handle it?" I repeated.

"Do you want me to send a memo around or something?"

"A memo?"

"A *memo,*" she enunciated, "to tell people it was another Jo-Ann Foote who passed away. That you're still alive."

"People aren't going to confuse me with a sixy-three-year-old schoolteacher."

Maggie shrugged. She was twenty-two. "What did you want then?"

"A reaction, I guess."

"It's weird. But not that weird. I grew up with a Foote family in Springfield. You're not the only one." She looked at the obituary page, still open on my desk. "Jo Ann E. Foote," she murmured, shaking her head with what looked like regret. I closed the paper and said we both had work to do.

I checked with my mother almost daily over the next week to see if she had been offered condolences. "No one's mentioned it," she always said.

I stopped asking friends if they had seen my obituary. Too many said, "I get the *Times*." Or, "Oh, right . . . I *did* see that." In time the obituary evolved into a clever story over cocktails. I told it at parties—the icebreaker I had always wanted—and entertained new acquaintances doing voices: my mother ("I had the worst fright."); my secretary ("I'll put out a memo.").

"How bizarre," these strangers said. "How awful for you."

Then I met George from Marketing at a new-products reception. He listened to my story thoughtfully; I moved to the kicker for the sure, final laugh, repeating in my friends' slightly superior tone that *they,* after all, read the *Times.*

George didn't respond in the way I had come to expect. He opened his eyes a little wider, still not smiling, and said quietly, "I knew her. She was my fifth-grade teacher."

"Oh, no," I said.

"The nicest woman I ever met. . . ."

"I didn't know—"

"A saint. She baked us cookies. Bought Halloween stickers

with her own money. And never once complained about her leg braces." He shook his head with reverence and sorrow.

"I feel terrible," I said.

"Don't," said George, grinning. "Let's dance."

He talked the whole time, and I could feel his lips touching my hair. "I can usually keep that kind of thing up for much longer," he said "With someone else I might have talked about how the late Miss Foote sent me dollar bills for carfare when I was away at college, and how I was one of her pallbearers. But I caved early. I thought you were going to cry."

"Serves me right," I said.

"Now, now," George said, and asked if I were involved with anyone besides him.

Monday morning, Maggie buzzed me in her blandest voice and said there was a kid with some flowers and did I want her to tip him?

"Who are they for?"

"Miss Foote," a male voice said.

"Please," I said. "And bring them right in."

A bored Maggie came through my door with a bouquet of white lilies. "Somebody die?" she asked.

When I lowered the bunch to smell them, I saw a single pink sweetheart rose nestled in the center. The gift card was white with a gold cross in one corner. "To Miss Foote," it said, "from George." The handwriting was a childish scrawl with a few letters written backwards.

I sent Maggie for an office vase and propped the card against my telephone, smiling in the privacy of my office.

Maybe I had a boyfriend now, a funny boyfriend who made impetuous gestures. Maybe he was thinking of me with his feet up on his desk and the faraway smile of perfume commercials on his face. If you didn't count wrist corsages at Sadie Hawkins dances, these were my first unsolicited flowers.

Maggie came back with a vase, and I tried to look like someone with a secret admirer. She didn't say a word.

"Sorry to let my personal life interfere with your work," I said.

She looked surprised, even annoyed, as if to say that one delivery of flowers hardly constituted a personal life.

"That'll be all," I said. She picked up the card.

"George," she read. "A guy."

I thought of sending one of those printed thank-yous through the interoffice mail—that the family of Jo-Ann Foote gratefully acknowledges your kind expression of sympathy—but I couldn't judge its cleverness. I dialed his extension instead.

"May I say who's calling?" a secretary asked—so sweetly that I wanted to hang up and fire Maggie.

"Jo-Ann," I told her.

George's voice boomed hello in seconds.

"Thank you for the lovely flowers."

"Your hair sure smells nice," he answered.

I asked if he could join me for dinner Saturday night—home-made pasta to say thank you.

"I can't, but I'm free Thursday."

Thursday. "Let me get back to you," I said.

I hung up and redialed. "Please," I said to the sweet voice. "I can't remember George's wife's name, and I knew you could help."

"Who is this?" she asked.

"It's just for my place cards. I'm his attorney's wife."

"Mr. Fitzgerald is divorced," she said with quiet dignity.

"Of course. How silly. My husband filed the papers."

"Shall I say you called, Mrs. . . . ?"

"Don't you dare," I said as coyly as I knew how.

George continued to woo me in his confident, easy style: good-night and good-morning phone calls; greeting cards and bouquets of Mylar balloons, which reminded me of the late Miss Foote. I got fitted for a diaphragm and had my first honeymoon cystitis ever. George brought his plants to my apartment, then his cat, finally his personal computer. One night, we talked about the '88 Olympics as an event we'd be viewing together.

He often said he was surprised that I'd never married. I told him I had given up at twenty-eight, twenty-nine, thirty, again at thirty-six, and for good lately.

"Ever come close?" he asked.

Of course I said I had. I embellished my former relationships just enough so that I had myself returning a few fraternity pins and losing deposits on a few function rooms. George believed me to be attractive, even desirable, the kind of woman who actually ends relationships herself. It was true that I had lately been considered attractive in a myopic, narrow-shouldered way, where as a girl I was just considered gawky, but not to the Georges of the world, not to the class presidents, even at my best.

I needed to hear about his life, particularly about his marriage, to see what made him turn to a Jo-Ann Foote. I guessed from his friends' excessive kindness toward me that his wife had been beautiful and accomplished, perhaps difficult to live with, but poised and charming.

If only I could see a photograph.

When we had been dating for several months, I heard from her, or at least from a woman I deduced to be his wife. My phone rang late one night, and a pleasant female voice asked if I were Jo-Ann Foote.

"Yes," I said.

"The one who used to teach at Pinehurst Middle School?"

"I certainly am not."

"Oh," said the caller. "Are you a relative of hers?"

"No," I said, turning phrases around in my head, wondering if it were my place to announce the bad news.

"You sound like her," said the pleasant voice.

"Miss Foote passed away in November. Her obituary was in the *Globe.*"

"Darn," said my caller.

"Sorry to be the one to tell you," I said, lying; I was annoyed by the implication that I had the voice of a retired schoolteacher.

"Does this happen a lot?" she asked.

"Who are you?" I asked.

She hung up. I couldn't fall back to sleep, worrying about how I sounded—even how I looked. Of course it had to be George's ex-wife. He must have said, "I'm seeing someone," and she said *Who?* and he said "Jo-Ann Foote," and she said, "How'd you meet her?" and he told her. Maybe she wanted to hear George in the background, or wanted to see if I sounded the way pretty women do over the phone—breathless and distracted.

I had never asked George for the details, even when he sat back grinning, the happy listener, a newly opened bottle of dark beer poised at his lips, as I talked about a lifetime of disastrous blind dates. He was amused rather than disturbed by my history, by the men I had dated who brought me along to family dinners for years in place of their gay lovers; the others who escorted me to parties and sent me home in taxis after meeting hotter numbers; and the never-ending stream of friends' cast-off lovers, newly separated co-workers, and dating-service perennials. George hardly knew of the underbelly of single life. It amazed him that there was a subculture of people who didn't like themselves or their lives.

"C'mon," he'd say. "You actually signed up with a dating service! I can't believe it."

Then I'd have to tell him again about my three referrals—my three insurance company middle-managers; our evenings out and our conversations about their first marriages, joint custody, health clubs, est, and water beds.

"Did you ever go out with any of them again?" George asked.

"No!" I said, failing to confess that the middle one was actually quite nice and that I would have if asked.

"Lots of very respectable people sign up for dating services," I told him. "After all, what are the alternatives for people our age?"

George looked startled as if I were the first human to identify such a dilemma.

Months passed, and George stayed with me. He rented a parking space in my building and sublet his condo. He visited my office often, flirted with me through the intercom as he perched on the edge of Maggie's desk. We held hands openly. Maggie's mood improved and her episodes of insubordination diminished.

"I like George," she announced one day. "He's all right. And he's certainly got a thing for you."

"Do you think it's 'a thing'?" I asked. "Was that phrasing deliberate? Or do you see it as a relationship?"

Maggie closed the door to my office and pulled up a chair. "Amy says it's true love," she said in a low voice. Amy was George's secretary—a friendship Maggie had recently cultivated.

"How can you tell?"

"She says he never had anyone's picture on his desk before. Even Katherine's."

"I see." Katherine.

"And he's always in a good mood."

"That's something new?"

"From what she says."

"I hope you're being discreet," I told her.

"Hey—I don't want to blow it any more than you do. This is the best thing that ever happened to us." Maggie smiled. *Us.* She had never used pronouns like that to describe our relationship.

"Good," I said. "Thank you."

She stood up and pushed the chair back in place. There was something so precise and neat about the way she patted the furniture and closed the door behind her; something so secretarial.

Bolstered by Amy's report via Maggie, I finally asked George about his ex-wife. He told me, surprised that I was interested, about her being a pretty nice woman with a good business sense.

"Do you mind if I ask what went wrong?"

"Wrong?" he said, as if he hadn't given it much thought. "Oh . . . one of those things, I guess. College sweethearts . . . married young . . . women's liberation . . . the usual . . ."

"Was it very hard?" I asked. "The divorce?"

"I suppose," he said. Then, "Not really."

"I'm very curious about her. I don't even know her name."

"Katherine," said George. "I never mentioned her name? In all these months?"

I shook my head.

"Anything else?" he asked.

"Kids?" I asked.

"Of course not," he said. "I certainly would have told you if I had kids."

"That's what I thought."

"I love kids," he said. "Katherine didn't want any."

"Oh," I said.

"You want kids, don't you?" George asked. "You like kids, right?"

"Love them."

"Good," said George.

"What does Katherine look like?" I asked.

"Pretty," he said. "Pretty and skinny. Athletic, though. Nice body."

"Is she dark? Light?"

"Reddish hair. Greenish eyes. Very all-American looking."

"I'm sick," I told Maggie later.

Just before my Friday lunch date with George, Maggie buzzed me and said in a strangely formal voice that I had guests.

"Send them in," I told her.

"You come out," George called. And I knew.

He had brought Katherine to meet me, just like that. He introduced us with an oblivious grin and the wave of a casual forefinger: Jo-Ann Foote . . . Katherine Fitzgerald. We shook hands and I stared.

"Katherine works downtown," George said, as if that explained everything.

"Lovely to meet you," said Katherine confidently. "George insisted."

Maggie made an obscene gesture only I could see.

"Where shall we go?" asked George. "Anyone feel like oysters?"

We took his suggestion. The maître d' sat us at a table for four, with George next to me and Katherine opposite him where I could stare from a different angle. She said she had heard how we'd met—the obituary; George pretending to know the other Miss Foote, the one who died. His asking me to *dance* in the middle of my confusion. Such a sweet story.

George squeezed my narrow shoulders and said I was a good sport, a very good sport.

"I should *say*," murmured Katherine.

A waiter brought a second bottle of wine and gave George the first taste. I asked Katherine where she worked, and she seemed surprised I had to ask. "I'm a fabric designer—hand-painted cottons and silks."

I took in the life-size birds on her white cossack shirt. "Is that one of yours?" I asked.

She held out both arms proudly. "'*Les oiseaux dans la neige.*'"

George prodded my empty oyster shells with his fork, rummaging for any morsels I might have overlooked.

"Order some more," Katherine snapped. "You don't have to scrounge around her plate."

"Jo-Ann doesn't mind. She's used to it." He leaned sideways to bump my shoulder, like two glasses clinking in a toast. No one acknowledged the lone fat oyster, untouched and glistening on Katherine's plate.

Katherine explained to George exactly why lunch should be her treat—the pleasure of meeting me; a deal with Japan signed that very morning for *beaucoup* yen. The busboy cleared our table as she made her case, and I watched our empty shells make their final trip back to the kitchen. "Let her," I said, thinking fondly of the leftover osyter, grateful it hadn't given its life in vain.

Keeping in Touch with Holly

My mother and Mrs. Durant see each other in the neighborhood and still swap news about their daughters. This has been going on for twenty years, since Holly and I were teenagers, when our mothers would sigh with false exasperation over our boy worshipping and our grand ambitions. Now it is the conversation of two elderly women discussing unmarried daughters: our promotions; our condominiums; where we last vacationed. It is a competition of sorts, at least on my mother's part; a grudge that builds with time. She wants concrete reasons for my failure to remain anyone's wife and produce grandchildren, and the thing she has chosen to blame is Holly's example.

We were best friends for one year in high school—Holly's last and my junior year—when her parents divorced and she was recalled from prep school to keep her mother company. I was a year younger than Holly and a shade paler in all the important areas: boys, grades, college catalogue collections. Holly adopted me as her confidante, teaching me how to flirt; reforming me. She chose me when she returned to town, needing a friend at the public high school. I was smart and popular in an unconscious way, and I was eager to learn.

Holly was already a legend by Labor Day of her senior year because she made cheerleader over the summer, even before her transfer was official. More remarkably, she withdrew before school started and gave her spot to the alternate, saying she had tried out for the fun of it but had no intention of doing cartwheels in front of horny high school boys and freezing her ass off. That's what I admired about Holly, her swearing in a rude way, all the while taking Advanced Placement English and Honors Biology. She drove her mother's car with great assurance, one wrist doing it all, and often with older boys home from college riding in the back seat. It was during one such ride that she pulled up next to me at the bus stop and said, "Why don't you give me a call." I did, of course, immediately and was invited to visit. Her house was large and modern, with many levels and rough pine walls, like an elegant version of a cabin in Vermont. Set on a wooded lot, the only one for blocks around, it overlooked our neighborhood. It had been her parents' dream house, designed by a famous architect. Holly's room had built-in shelves and drawers and one entire wall of cork.

She cross-examined me that afternoon and I knew by the time I left that I had passed her disciple test: my taste ran to penny loafers but not necessarily ones made in Maine; I smoked cigarettes occasionally but coughed when I inhaled. Beginning that night, Holly telephoned me after dinner and we talked about things personal and sexual.

"I've decided to like Michael Ahern," she announced.

"Which one is he?"

"Pamela Downey's boyfriend? He didn't wait for her after calculus today. He applied early admission to Amherst."

"What are you going to do?"

"I'll call him tonight and ask him about the assignment. Tomorrow I'll give him a note before class."

"Saying what?"

"'Thanks for your help last night.' Or, 'Hope I didn't call too late. Did you mind?' That'll plant the idea in his head that I'm interested, then he can make the next move."

Next Friday night, Holly would be at the varsity basketball game with Michael Ahern. Saturday morning she'd call and describe his kissing technique.

On the basis of my end of these conversations, my mother said Holly was boy-crazy. "You haven't done anything with Roberta for a long time. Or Celeste. They're such nice girls."

Looking back, I see that Holly was a nice girl, too, and that I could have challenged my mother's insinuation, but at sixteen I wasn't on firm ground discussing my new friend's character. She was missing the layer of humility that made others look polite and sweet. She could raise her hand in class and ask what, exactly, the purpose of an assignment was, or compliment a young male teacher on the color of his eyes. Once, in order to sneak a cigarette in the middle of class, Holly lowered her half-slip a good six inches below her hemline, walked past the young male substitute teacher, and left with a smile only we could see.

The half-slip made her famous. Michael Ahern was dismissed for Forrest Whittaker, a three-letter man and National Merit semifinalist. Michael Ahern asked me out and I went. His occasional letters from Bowdoin the next year always ended with, "What's Holly up to?" or "You still in touch with Holly?"

I barely stayed in touch with her when she went to the University of Pennsylvania. She checked in with me during her school vacations, and picked up our conversations where they had left off. Where was I applying? My safety school? Who was I in love with and how far had we gone?

She announced that she had finally done it and was unofficially pinned. She had not enjoyed the first two times, but was now enthusiastic and using protection. His name was Sven and he was a double major, history and economics. He had technique, Holly told me. He was a senior.

I had gone back to Roberta and Celeste after apologizing for my desertion. I was the bold, popular one who targeted shy boys and organized Friday night sixsomes. We met in Roberta's finished basement, put a little rum in our Cokes, and danced close to Gerry and the Pacemakers. Sometimes I called boys and asked for assignments, and sometimes I handed them notes before class. Always they were good students, and without exception they wore chinos and penny loafers. Holly had taught me how to look for the tiny notch on the instep that certified the make as Weejuns.

I talked about Holly when I got to college, about her nerve, as we called it then. We were always looking for ways to find boyfriends, and Holly's techniques were admired and emulated. "Is she pretty?" most people asked after hearing of her successes. Holly *was* pretty, but it seemed beside the point. "Very sure of herself," I'd say. "Lots of confidence. Her looks are secondary."

I was the leading practitioner of Holly's techniques in my circle, placing long-distance calls to hometown boys at good colleges, and proposing platonic weekends together. I wrote letters to get letters, and opened these ceremoniously in class, hoping others would notice the return addresses from Middlebury or Hanover or Palo Alto.

I invited Holly to visit me for a weekend my junior year. She drove up from Philadelphia with an extremely thin young man who wore a long woolen scarf around his neck despite the warm spring weather. Holly kissed him good-bye at my dorm, thanked him for the ride, and wished him a superb weekend.

"Jonathan's a homosexual," she told me, "His lover's at Harvard." I had fashionable people for her to meet; I had prepared casual references to Ivy League sex and updated the museum prints tacked to my dorm walls. But in those days everything sophisticated seemed sophomoric next to close homosexual friends.

I gave her a choice of graduate school mixers for Friday night and dinner first at a new crêperie.

"Where can we get bleacher seats for the Red Sox game?" Holly asked.

The bleachers were filled with young men without dates. Holly led me to a spot behind a promising candidate—broad shoulders in pink oxford cloth; boat shoes without socks. "I disagree," she announced suddenly in her clear, assured voice. "Undergraduates don't have sunburned necks this time of year." His shoulders straightened. "And the shirt," Holly continued. "Most guys in college don't have the self-confidence to wear pink, especially to a ball game. I'd say twenty-five, twenty-six." Pink Shirt shifted in his seat.

A few innings passed. Holly appeared to be concentrating on the game. "What's that called?" she asked me in a loud voice. I stared at her blankly. "You know—when the ball goes into the stands, but it bounces on the field first?"

"I forget," I said.

"Damn! It's on the tip of my tongue."

Pink Shirt turned around. He grinned when he saw who was asking. "Ground-rule double," he said, and introduced himself.

My friends and I followed the Red Sox schedule and returned once every home stand to try our luck. We selected places behind collegiate-looking backs and spoke our lines. I took the Holly role and made sunburned-neck observations—that undergraduates don't smoke imported cigarettes or drink black coffee or, on a lucky night, wear pink. But as we tired of our results—freshmen from Wentworth Institute who taught us to fill in our scorecards—the legend of Holly and her pink-shirted law student, whose neck turned out to be bronzed from Olympic rowing, grew and grew.

I graduated in 1968. Girls were married right out of college then, and it seemed to me that I was the only member of my class without a diamond glinting in the sun of our outdoor commencement. I won a prize for the graduating senior majoring in education whose qualities of mind and spirit most closely resembled those of the late Ida Marguerite Prescott, class of 1912. My hometown paper ran my picture, and several school superintendents called with job offers. I took the highest bid and began my lesson plans.

The announcement also brought a graduation card from Holly's mother. "Why don't you get in touch with her?" she wrote, supplying a Cambridge phone number and address. Why doesn't she get in touch with me? I asked the signature, and put the card aside.

School brought new boyfriends. I particularly enjoyed the Victorian custom of addressing current lovers as "Mr. Howe" or "Mr. Leone" as we passed in the corridors. I lived at home as did my teacher boyfriends. We saw movies and ate club sandwiches several towns away to avoid our students on weekends. The following September, a new crop of well-dressed, pretty college grads joined the staff and were given the rush by my teacher-suitors. I called Holly. "You're psychic," she said. "I'm having a party Saturday night. Come."

I wore a dark cotton peasant skirt and a black leotard, carefully selected for my evening in Cambridge. Holly introduced me as her oldest friend. We drank wine and passed occasional joints around. There were many more men than women. Holly worked in the law school library, and I could see what fertile social ground it was. Her friends formed admiring circles around her as she performed her hostess chores. No one seemed to mind the disproportions of the guest list.

"You are, by far, the most interesting man here," I heard her tell one guest.

Her intimacy was contagious. I slipped my arm around a few waists, too, and confessed I picked them out from all the rest. After much wine, I kissed some appealing mouths in the middle of conversation, and apologized for my spontaneity.

On Monday morning in the teachers' room, for no particular reason, I slipped my arm around my department chairman's waist. "Good morning, Henry," I said. It was a small school in a small town. I was not invited to the department Christmas party at his home, and all the gym teachers—his wife's co-workers—stopped speaking to me. When my name came up before the school committee two years later, I didn't get tenure. The fact that it was Holly's fault made no difference to anyone but me.

There were very few men in my graduate program, and we single women had them catalogued by the end of the welcome luncheon. Lawrence was the only real possibility, and I took the empty seat next to his in "Indexing and Abstracting." Close up, he was quite ordinary looking, except for high cheekbones and wild eyebrows. His shirt was a red and white gingham, with mother-of-pearl snaps; his cardigan sweater had stains at the cuffs. Sweet, I thought. Just before class ended I scribbled a note: "Do you *get* this?"

Lawrence read it carefully and took a long time composing his answer.

"I think I do," it said.

"Could I call you if I get stuck?" I wrote back.

He nodded eagerly and gave me his phone number. I called that night. He answered after exactly two rings, sounding determinedly baritone. I was twenty-five, and it felt like I had been doing this a very long time.

My parents put our engagement notice in my hometown paper. "Librarians affianced," announced the headline. Lawrence and I were married at the MIT chapel, exercising his alumni privileges. The department gave us a tea and said we were the seventeenth M.L.S. marriage since records were kept. And none easier than this, I thought.

Holly's mother must have sent her the wedding announcement, because I heard from her promptly. "Egad!" and "Holly" were all that the card said. Her gift was a paperback book on the small inns of New England—not what I expected from the guiding force behind my marriage.

Lawrence and I signed up as a team with the placement office. Prospective employers liked the wholesomeness of us, the very two-ness of the package. We left Boston in June for a remote New Hampshire campus where we worked days, and at night watched New Hampshire Public Television. Sometimes other librarians had dinner parties, and sometimes one of the youngish professors using my archives invited us to brunch. We had an open-house one Sunday in January for some staff and faculty who stayed on between semesters. A good half-hour after everyone else had gone, Judd Maloney of the English Department came with a bottle of Spanish champagne.

"Where's *Mrs.* Maloney?" Lawrence asked, squinting into the snow and dark from our front door.

"Mrs. Maloney is with her parents in New Jersey, planning our divorce," he said festively.

"Tough break," said Lawrence.

"Actually not," said Judd. "Is your corkscrew handy?"

Judd sat on the couch and smiled a frank smile at me until Lawrence returned. He filled three glasses with the Spanish champagne. "This is quite good, and ridiculously cheap," Judd said.

"Delicious," we murmured.

"So who'd I miss?" asked Judd.

"Almost nobody," I said.

"I thought I'd come fashionably late and hit the singles' constituency."

"There wasn't one," I said.

"Too bad some of my co-workers didn't stay. I work with several very nice single women," Lawrence said.

Judd smiled faintly. "A damn shame."

Lawrence rose, and offered Judd cheese and crackers. "You can always drop by the circulation desk and take your pick," he called from the kitchen.

Judd arched one black-Irish eyebrow. "I already have," he said in the undertone we used in the archives.

By the time the class notes arrived in the mail, announcing our marriage and joint appointment, Lawrence and I were living apart. Neither one of us set the record straight for many years—odd for librarians—until Lawrence met another alumna and sent a cutely worded engagement announcement to *Biblio-file.* Our class secretary called long-distance to say that some facts were missing, such as what had happened to me. "She picked up another man in the stacks and we got divorced," said Lawrence. "You can write whatever you want."

Judd Maloney and I did not turn into anything reportable once the obstacle of Lawrence had been removed. Judd continued to murmur the kind of compliments for which women leave their husbands, but louder and louder until he tossed them about jovially at the circulation desk and I realized it was just his way.

Before this last Thanksgiving, I sent Holly a note with the dates of my homecoming. "Any chance you're getting away from it all for a (groan) quiet weekend, too?" I wrote, imagining us co-hostesses of a party for the old crowd. Mrs. Durant called my mother to say it was Santa Barbara this year—Holly's new boyfriend was a physicist and presenting a paper there—but she might drop in at Christmas.

"I can't pretend I'm sorry to have you to myself," my mother admitted. "Besides, don't you think you've outgrown her kind of foolishness?"

We ate turkey sandwiches on tray tables Thanksgiving night and watched Richard Harris in *Camelot.* I went to bed early and pretended to be asleep when my mother tiptoed in to turn off my lamp. Even after all these years, I looked up the hill to see whose lights were out first—another game Holly started, a habit I cannot break.

A Daughter Your Age

At parties, it helps when Marybeth mentions that she works for 'PBX. She has the quiet, plain manner of one who programs computers or peers into a microscope for a living, so the revelation that she works in radio, public radio, shocks most new men into eye contact. They do not expect the details of her life to be any more interesting than her appearance, which hasn't departed much from her parochial-school dress code. At twenty-five, Marybeth worries that her virginity, like her long-sleeved cotton blouses and woolen jumpers, is a style she can't update.

Marybeth is unhappy at work—disillusioned with the institution she so admired through her headphones. It has not turned out to be the friendly, altruistic place which once inspired her annual pledges. She was surprised to be hired at all after her interview with Thea, now her boss.

"What do you do when you're not working?" Thea asked.

Marybeth recited the activities listed on her résumé under Personal Interests. Thea laughed, making Marybeth jump. "Gotcha! You were supposed to say, 'Classical music and "All Things Considered."'"

"Of course," Marybeth said.

"Too late!" Thea sang. "What else should I know about you?"

"I speak French. I meet deadlines."

"What are you? Married, single, divorced?"

"Single. Why?"

"I hope you don't have any illusions about this being a good place to meet men. It ain't a glamorous job. It's churning out a helluva lot of words for lousy pay."

A week later Thea told Marybeth over the phone in a bored, flat voice—calling her Mary Ann—that she had the job.

"Thank you very much," Marybeth said. "I'll do a good job for you."

Thea groaned. "How old are you anyway?"

"Twenty-five."

"You look even younger. I have a daughter twenty-five. She's always falling in love with the wrong man."

"I see," Marybeth said politely.

On her first day, she learned she was Thea's second choice. The favored candidate was a young man with on-air experience and, Marybeth gathered, more charisma. He turned Thea down.

"You're going to have to win me over. I like outrageous people." Thea looked her up and down, then exchanged glances with Janine, her secretary, whose head was shaven and whose mouth was twisted into a habitual smirk. Noon passed, then one o'clock, with no one suggesting a welcome-aboard lunch or even a tour of the vending machines.

Thea has been as noisy and brash a boss as her interviewing techniques promised. She edits Marybeth's press releases in magenta ink with great slashes and margin queries, inserting exclamation points between Marybeth's quiet sentences. From time to time, when she admires a bit of writing, Thea asks Marybeth if it's original. It is the closest thing to praise she hears from the woman who hired her.

Marybeth doesn't know how or when to acquire outrageousness. She is intimidated by reports that her predecessor, a young Canadian named Jacques who released primal screams at his typewriter and kept condoms in his desk, was much admired. Marybeth works at just being heard over the din of Thea and Janine's conversations. She wishes she didn't have to look up when Thea bursts from her office every few hours to try out a manic headline on Janine.

"Seiji is delicious!" she yells.

"Great," Janine mutters.

"Shall we go with it?"

"Isn't it a little undignified for 'Live from Symphony Hall'?" ventures Marybeth.

Thea glares and marches back into her office. Later, in a scrawled memorandum, she explains to Marybeth that what public radio needs is more irreverence and less "dignity"—enclosed in quotes as if the very word is contemptible.

Marybeth learns that Thea is divorced from a Yale professor who writes about DNA for lay readers. She favors jokes about their former sex life, about his new wife and *their* sex life, and about her own bouts with romance. She is fond of sight gags, too. When a good-looking man confers with Thea in her office, she closes the door behind him, with a leer for Janine. As a variation, she opens her door mid-meeting and kicks her shoes into the outer office. This is Thea's outrageousness. She is six feet tall, lanky, with hair hennaed the color of dried apricots.

Thea invites Marybeth to lunch one Friday and takes her to a neighborhood bar.

"My daughter's your age," Thea announces over mugs of beer she had ordered for them both.

"You mentioned that."

"She's a gorgeous kid. Too gorgeous."

"How can anyone be too gorgeous?" Marybeth asks.

Thea smiles proudly. "She's a brat. She uses people. She makes dates with two different men for the same night and goes out with whoever shows first." Thea raises her beer in a toast. "And you know what? The jerk who gets left behind usually comes back for more."

"Wow," says Marybeth.

"I bet your mother has no complaints."

"Thank you."

"No—I mean, you don't strike me as the type who talks back."

Marybeth tries to affect a look and tone of nonchalance. "We don't fight. We don't particularly talk, either."

Thea arches her eyebrows. "Oh?"

"She's disappointed in me. When I got my own apartment, she assumed it was to commit mortal sins in. She goes to Mass every day and worries I won't be with her for eternity."

"Fascinating," Thea says.

"If not ironic," Marybeth adds, then blushes.

Thea stares at her new employee's heart-shaped, freckled face. "Your hair is quite an attractive color," is all she says.

Later, alone with Janine, Marybeth asks her what she's doing wrong.

"Just relax," she answers.

"I don't think she likes me, though."

Janine closes her eyes. "Thea likes balls. Just talk back once in a while."

"Be more assertive?"

"Yeah."

"I'm not actually shy. Just reserved. There's a difference."

"If you say so."

"I mean, I'm willing to change. It hasn't gotten me very far being . . . unassertive." Her voice trails off as she ponders the social liabilities of being quiet—presumed shy—and the sexual milestones still before her. Thea walks in and Marybeth greets her with an energetic hello. Janine follows Thea into her private office and shuts the door behind them both.

Marybeth meets a man at a friend's Halloween party. The only two not in costume, they are wearing white shirts with the same camel-brown pinstriping. He is handsome, she thinks, in a neat, parochial-school way.

"What do you do?" he asks.

"I'm in radio."

His face lights up. "Where?"

"WPBX?" she murmurs.

"No kidding." He grins and extends his hand. "Third floor. Development. We're co-workers."

Marybeth immediately worries that Kenneth, as an insider, won't succumb to her one mystique—working in public broadcasting. But he returns to her side after refilling his drink and again after feeding his meter. Before the party is over, he is steering Marybeth through the crowd with his hand politely but proprietarily at the small of her back. When they part, he carefully spells her last name.

"I hope we'll see each other again," Marybeth tells him, remembering to be assertive.

Monday morning he telephones from Development and asks her to a basketball game for the following Friday. She accepts and smiles happily for several minutes after hanging up. "That was Kenneth," she announces to no one in particular. Thea appears.

"Who?"

"Someone I met at a party this weekend." Marybeth cocks her head toward the phone and smiles. "He just called."

Janine groans.

"What's your problem?" Thea snaps.

"Is he going to ask her to the hop, too?"

Thea laughs appreciatively. She curls her fist into an imaginary microphone and croons, "'A white sport coat, and a pink carnation. . . .'" Janine jumps to her feet and dances from side to side.

"The *stroll!*" Thea shrieks. She kicks off her shoes and joins Janine. "Sing, Marybeth. Something late Fifties-ish."

Marybeth's throat tightens. Thea and Janine dance in place as if waiting for a cue. "I don't know any songs," she says.

"Sing," Thea says, "or you're fired."

"You're a bitch, Thea," Janine says, still dancing. Thea laughs and twirls.

"You can stop hyperventilating, Marybeth," Thea tells her. "This is what's known as having fun."

Marybeth smiles uncertainly.

"Go ahead, laugh."

"Thea—" Marybeth begins.

"I mean it. I want to hear you laugh a real goddamned laugh."

Marybeth forces a shallow laugh.

"That's pathetic. Stand up."

Conditioned by the sisters at Saint Catherine's, Marybeth stands.

"Up! Stand up on the desk and laugh for us."

"Tell a joke," Janine suggests. "Maybe she'd laugh at a joke." Marybeth lowers herself slowly to her seat and swivels to face the typewriter. She feels the two women exchanging glances, and hears footsteps retreating. Thea's door closes.

"It was just a joke," Janine says after a while.

At home in her apartment, Marybeth practices her laugh. It reminds her of novitiates from *The Sound of Music* tittering behind their fingers. A "Monty Python" rerun fails to elicit any spontaneous laughter, so she shuts off the TV and laughs into her cassette recorder. The results sound forced. She rewinds several minutes of tape and tries again, picturing Kenneth next to her on the bleachers, leaning close to make his clever words heard over the noise of the crowd. She raises her chin and shakes her hair in what she thinks is a laugh of abandon. I love your laugh, Kenneth might say. It suits you.

Marybeth brings her sandwich to the cafeteria and sees Thea at a table in the center of the room. She is with a young woman Marybeth doesn't recognize. A job interview, Marybeth thinks. I've walked in on her interviewing my replacement. Thea looks up and waves.

"My daughter," she yells, pointing.

Not gorgeous, Marybeth thinks, just stunning. The auburn hair was probably the inspiration for her mother's bottled color. She is thin and fashionably dressed in an oversized sweater of some gleaming yarn.

"Come *here*," Thea shouts. Her daughter smiles a brief smile over her shoulder in Marybeth's direction. "Tammy . . . Marybeth."

"Oh, that's right," says Tammy. "Jacques' replacement." And to Marybeth: "What an outrageous guy."

"Tammy worked with me last summer," her mother explains.

"What did you do before you came to 'BPX?" Tammy asks.

As Marybeth answers in careful detail, Tammy surveys the cafeteria and bestows smiles on her old summer friends.

Thea asks Marybeth to lunch—an act of conciliation, she thinks, for ordering her to perform foolish tricks. Janine joins them. "How's the romance going?"

"Fine."

"What's this guy like?" Janine asks.

Marybeth thinks of saying, "You know him. He works at the station." But the image of all four of them riding in the elevator—Thea and Janine *knowing*—squelches the impulse.

"He's not your type," Marybeth answers.

"Well, well, well," Thea says.

Janine persists. "How'd you meet this guy?"

"At a party. Last weekend."

"I know. I mean, how did you two get it on?"

Marybeth smiles, thinking of their matching pinstripes. She sips her wine and swallows deliberately.

"I saw him . . . liked him . . . asked him to dance."

"Well, well," Thea repeats.

Marybeth nods. "He likes assertive women."

"Does he know you're a virgin?" asks Thea.

I should quit right now, Marybeth thinks. Stand up, pay my share, leave a tip, and walk out. Let her explain it to Personnel. Let her write the press releases for the Christmas programming.

Thea hails the waiter. "Two black coffees," she says when

he arrives. And adds, "One tea." To Marybeth, it sounds like an apology.

Friday night after the basketball game, Marybeth invites Kenneth back to her apartment for coffee. They talk about the station and people they know in common. Marybeth asks if he knows why Janine is bald.

He tells her he has heard that she shaves her head because her cranium is unusually symmetrical, and that she bleaches the stubble to achieve total whiteness. "Something like that," Kenneth says.

"I believe it."

"A sculptor recommended she do it."

"I hate it," says Marybeth. "I have to look at it all day long."

"Quite a team, those two."

"You wouldn't believe how they talk to each other."

"Janine's been her secretary for life."

"They think I'm uptight," Marybeth says. "They're trying to convert me."

Kenneth nods grimly. "Typical Thea."

"She hates me. I'm not cool enough for public broadcasting."

He laughs. "Did you say *cruel*? You're not cruel enough for public broadcasting? That could be." Thea's not even the worst of the lot, Kenneth tells her. She's talented, in a hysterical way; she has a human side.

"And a daughter my age," Marybeth says.

"I know," he answers.

"Do you think I'm nervous?" Marybeth asks.

"Not really."

"What would you say if I told you that I've never slept with anyone?"

"I'd say I'm not totally surprised."

"Are you surprised I brought it up?"

"I'm flattered."

"I'm practicing being straightforward. Thea and Janine think I need assertiveness training."

Kenneth kisses Marybeth gently. "Positive reinforcement," he says. Before he leaves, Kenneth mentions a movie he'd like to see the following Saturday night.

"The twenty-ninth," she confirms. Marybeth takes his hand at the door. "We could have lunch together during the week." Go public, she thinks. Declare us an official office romance.

"Soon," says Kenneth.

When Marybeth gets to work Monday morning, Thea is pacing angrily in front of Janine's desk.

"They couldn't care less," Janine tells her. "They wouldn't miss our money. They wouldn't even notice." Thea stops to glare at Marybeth before rushing out and down the hall.

Marybeth asks Janine what's going on.

"The *Globe* panned our Oscar Wilde festival."

"That's it?"

"She wants to pull our advertising as punishment."

"That'll scare 'em," Marybeth says with a smile.

Janine stares, unsmiling, then speaks. "She had a bad weekend. Okay?"

As she boils water for her tea and sorts the morning's news

clips, Marybeth tries to figure it out. *Bad weekend for Thea.* An illness? A death? A man?

Thea returns and heads straight for Marybeth's desk. "And how are you this morning, Miss Marybeth? Happy?"

Marybeth looks up.

"One of these days you'll wake up and you won't be young and in love anymore. Or you'll be in love and he won't."

"Thee-a," Janine intones.

Thea glares at Janine and back at Marybeth before stalking into her office.

"She's crazy today," Marybeth whispers.

A few minutes pass, then Janine speaks in a detached monotone: "Some nice guy dumped her daughter. Someone Thea thought was good for Tammy and didn't take her crap."

Kenneth calls Marybeth before the morning is over and asks her to join him for lunch. "I'd love it," she answers, admiring her own breezy tone. Friday night, she thinks; now Monday for lunch and next Saturday, the twenty-ninth.

Kenneth meets her in the cafeteria at noon and leads her outside to a sunny spot on the station grounds. It is mild for November, and the brown grass is dry and warm. Marybeth rolls up her long sleeves and smiles into the sun with her eyes closed. In movies, she thinks, men kiss women at this point. Or trace their profiles with a blade of grass. Instead, Kenneth unwraps sandwiches and tries to keep the napkins from blowing away.

"Thea came to see me this morning," Marybeth hears him say. "I think we'd better talk."

The dreaded words: we'd better talk. She feels a stab of disappointment and a growing panic over the premature loss of so kind a first-time lover.

"I should have told you earlier," he says. "I used horrendous judgment."

No you didn't, she thinks. No one has ever been nicer.

"I had already decided to break up with her when I met you. I went to the party *knowing* I was breaking it off. And I did—this weekend."

"Thea?" Marybeth asks weakly. "Are you talking about Thea?"

"No! God, no," Kenneth says. "I mean Tammy, her daughter."

They stay outside for an hour, with Marybeth insisting she doesn't care if she is late. She hopes Thea is watching from the window and glancing at the clock. She wants Thea to see Kenneth stroke her bare forearm and pick the dead leaves off her clothes with such tenderness. Go get Janine and stare out the window together. See Kenneth bring his happy face close to mine and speak his clever words. Note how I throw my head back with such ease, and laugh.

Immediate Family

Background: Herb and Bianca got married, had fun with their joint incomes, and decided, no kids. It was the 1970s: they started a support group for nonparents and were named "nonparents of the year" at a national conference. Herb was quoted in a press release as saying that having children was the most insidious form of peer pressure; Bianca said, No, they weren't being selfish; no, she wouldn't regret it in her old age. They got a few years older, got restless, got unhappy, got divorced.

I am Herb's second wife. He is forty-seven, with grizzled hair on his chest and almost none on his head. Our children are four, three, and eighteen months. He is what our mothers affectionately call a crazy father.

Bianca is unmarried, childless, and ticking. She threatens to sue Herb for ruining her life. She is jealous of us, and particularly wild on the subject of Herb's ability to produce sperm regardless of age.

When I met Herb he was forty-two and much concerned with my fertility. "My first wife didn't want children," he offered practically as an introduction. I was thirty-one, and after we had sex for the first time he calculated that we had four years of childbearing before I needed amniocentesis. It was very much part of his appeal, his quest for a mother of his unborn children. Most men cared about my looks, or how I compiled aerobic points, or my capacity for giving and having orgasms. Only Herb asked if I planned to bottle- or breast-feed. I did not crave babies at the point we met, although I was generally in favor of them. Herb crystallized my goals. And why not: it wasn't as if he was looking for something bizarre and unnatural, or harboring unreasonable expectations. He wanted children and I wanted him.

My labor with all three was excruciating, and Herb didn't like the idea of anesthesia. When I was six centimeters dilated with Samantha, our first, and eligible for an epidural, Herb exhorted me to stick in there and tough it out. Our obstetrician, another football fan, bobbed his chin in agreement. I did tough it out. I also told a sobbing Herb as he held his newborn daughter that yes, it well may be the most beautiful moment of my life, but I'd never forgive his cavalier coaching. Not long after her birth, Herb passed a kidney stone and experienced terrific pain. "My labor was sixteen hours," I said unsympathetically. I switched obstetricians with Gabriel and Zachary and found someone who promised not to talk me out of painkillers.

Bianca has bought a condo less than two miles away since we've had the children. She is a consultant to businesses on how best to pipe music into their workplaces. She dresses only in black and white, which makes all the separate pieces of her wardrobe interchangeable. Her hair is professionally tinted to a perfect blue-black. She stays out of the sun so that her skin doesn't tan, and she dramatizes the effect with powder that makes her face unrealistically ivory. The only color she allows is Love That Red on her lips and fingernails. Herb thinks her post-divorce look is ghoulish and tells me she looks like Yvonne DeCarlo playing Lily on "The Munsters." That's his opinion. Women, I've noticed, stare at Bianca. I imagine them taking mental notes about the striking effect of her black-and-whiteness. While men stare, too, and frequently ask if they can call, none has stepped forward to marry Bianca or inseminate her with the child she claims so desperately to want.

She sends gifts to our three with cards signed "Aunt Bianca." I call her upon receipt (at first Herb did the calling) and ask that she limit her gift-giving to birthdays and Christmas. As the children get older they will ask for a definition of "Aunt" and we will have to say that she is not a sister of either parent, but Daddy's first wife (and sometimes marriages don't work out, people stop loving each other, blah blah blah, which will only make them nervous about Herb and me). Then, when they are mad at me they'll say, "Too bad Bianca's not our mother."

Her gifts, of course, are wonderful. Samantha was the first child in nursery school to have a bright-turquoise novelty necklace with plastic roller skates and other chunky charms hanging from its links. The boys get the expensive Dutch puzzles and German building blocks that can't be found at Toys-R-Us.

So why can't I just tell her to leave us alone if I'm threatened by all of this? Because Herb feels guilty.

"She left you," I remind him.

"A technicality," he answers. What happened was that Bianca packed a change of underwear and her toothbrush into an overnight bag and left for a weekend at her college roommate's to gain perspective and to experience missing Herb. She loved being away. No longing for home or Herb ever materialized.

"She cheated on you," I say.

Herb looks slightly aggrieved. He can't rationalize this one. He has told me he checked the night table when Bianca left and saw she had taken her diaphragm. The husband of the roommate had had a long-standing flirtation with Bianca—always joking about the sorority sister he *should* have married, ha ha ha—but Herb thought his type was all talk.

When his anger, if you can call it that, recedes, and I've accomplished nothing in terms of banishing Bianca, I edge closer to hysteria. "Fire me," I shout. "My work is done. Zachary is weaned to a cup. You have three beautiful children. Fire the surrogate mother and marry Bianca."

"I don't love Bianca. I love you," Herb says seriously.

How does she treat me? Vaguely and with *noblesse oblige*. I could be a new employee to whom she nods pleasantly while wondering which department I work in. I have read about a man's ex- and current wife sharing a bond. They have lunch together, share confidences, then when wife number two divorces him, the exes become roommates for the sake of all the half-siblings. Not Bianca and I.

Her threat of suing Herb arises every so often, but no lawyer she's ever dated thinks she has a case. We imagine she tells them how her ex-husband coerced her into staying childless, and the lawyers think "forced sterilization" and mentally get out their legal pads. But then Bianca takes out the yellow "nonparents-of-the-year" newspaper clippings. The lawyer undoubtedly reads Bianca's arrogant quotes, asks her if she really said all those things ("We love to travel—we've been known to jump into a taxi after work on Friday and catch the next flight to anywhere. Herb and I are spontaneous people."), and she says, "Yes, but I was brainwashed."

"Do you love to travel?" a good cross-examiner might ask. "Did you in fact jump in a taxi after work and take an unplanned vacation?"

"Once," Bianca would answer.

"Would you describe yourself as 'spontaneous'?" he might ask.

"His word," Bianca would testify.

Bianca's mother has no grandchildren. She hates Herb, Bianca tells him, with such passion that she could probably murder him and be acquitted by reason of temporary insanity.

"Why are you telling us this?" I ask Bianca.

"Herb liked my mother. I thought he'd be interested."

"What are we supposed to do?" I ask for the hundred-thousandth time. I recite my same old list of solutions: adoption, sperm banks, no-strings insemination by a casual partner. Bianca pooh-poohs each one with her familiar argument about the impersonality of it all.

"If you really wanted a child, you'd do it," I say. Bianca answers me with a stare. Her look says, you are naive and ignorant; I am a guest in your house so I won't speak with the contempt your statement deserves. She turns to Herb and says, "I snatched the Park 'N Shop account away from Muzak."

There is only one solution: ban her from my house. I begin my campaign by announcing to Herb that Bianca is not welcome for Thanksgiving.

"Okay," he says reasonably.

"She'll get another invitation."

"It's fine," he says.

"It's a good time to take a vacation. You could suggest that when you tell her we're only having the immediate family."

"Isn't the day before Thanksgiving the peak travel day of the whole year?" he asks.

"Hotels are empty, though."

"Whatever," says Herb.

"It's not really my problem," I say.

Herb agrees. Bianca has friends. Presumably, some will be having large Thanksgiving dinners. Why mention it at all, in fact? We say nothing. In early November, before I've ordered my turkey or decided on the pies, Bianca invites the five of us to her place for Thanksgiving. Herb accepts automatically, obediently.

Dinner is gorgeous: oysters and pistachios in the dressing; the salad tossed with raspberry vinegar and walnut oil; the bird browned to mahogany, moist in the breast and done at the joints. Except for the bowl of Kraft Macaroni and Cheese for the kids, it is *Gourmet* magazine's November menu. I supply the pies: store-bought apple and pumpkin. Our hostess tops them with her own crème fraîche.

Herb asks, "When did you learn to cook like this?"

"Like what?" Bianca answers, wide-eyed. The meal is over, yet her Love That Red looks undisturbed.

I ask Herb that night if he still has feelings for Bianca. "'Feelings' covers a lot of territory," he answers.

"Feelings of a sexual nature," I clarify.

At this juncture, most husbands would rush to deny any such thing. Not Herb. He is duty-bound to describe every nuance of every emotion just because I ask.

"Let me answer this way," he begins. "Bianca and I had no troubles sexually. It was other stuff that broke us up."

"So?" I ask.

"So of course there's some residual attraction. But I don't act on it."

I stew for a minute. "I thought you hated her new look."

Herb smiles a small smile.

"What?" I prompt.

"It's just like a woman to think men only sleep with perfect women. You go without if you don't like their fingernail color?"

"Are we talking about you and Bianca?" I ask.

"I meant, generically—does one go without if one objects merely to one aspect of a hypothetical woman's appearance?"

This is getting nowhere, except onto Herb's conversational flypaper. What I choose to retain is the tone of his voice—solemn, definite—when he said, "I don't act on it."

Bianca's mother calls with a proposal. She is a rich old lady who I picture in a lace widow's cap and caned wheelchair. I answer the phone to an imperious voice announcing that Dorothea Fendrick is calling for Herbert.

She wants to buy one of our children for Bianca. We can choose which one—a boy, most likely since we have two, and the baby would adjust the fastest—and we can see him whenever we want to. He would be told we were his aunt and uncle, and our children were his cousins. Financially, our children would never want.

I am furious at Herb for listening to more than the first four words of such a proposal. I want to call the police. He calls Bianca. "Mummy just rang us," he says wryly. "Can you guess about what?"

Bianca apparently hems and haws at the other end.

"Mummy thinks it would be nice if we gave one of the babies to you. We get to pick which one." He listens and shakes his head. "Sammy's our only girl. What's your second choice?" He listens some more and says, "Hold on a sec. I'll ask Lynn."

He covers the receiver with his palm. "What about Gabriel?" he asks.

If this were a joke, it occurs to me, he'd hold the phone up to my face so Bianca could hear my response. Coached, I would say, "For how much?" and Herb would say, "We're not that far apart. Let's counter." But that's not what he's doing. I say, "Hang up the phone." Herb opens his mouth to speak, but I grab the phone and yell, "Drop dead, Bianca."

Herb says he was having a little fun. Wouldn't I have enjoyed the look on her face when she came running over with a checkbook and we said it was all a joke?

"I don't see it that way," I say. I check the children and as I kiss each one think: imagine.

After a few days of my punishing him, Herb and I set down the terms: she can communicate only in writing and may not send presents to the children. Neither she nor her representatives may call Herb at work, or visit our house without notice; we also arrange for an unlisted number. If she violates our wishes, we will ask the courts for a temporary restraining order.

I make Herb recite the terms to her over the phone while I listen. To me, his voice sounds a little sing-song, as if he doesn't subscribe to what's being read.

He ends the conversation with, "See ya."

"She's ruining my life," I say.

"She took it very well," he answers.

"You take it very well, too. One might think you enjoyed our fighting over you."

"She doesn't want me," Herb says. Then: "She had her chance."

I tell him my friends' theory: "You're a new man, a father; crazy about your kids. That's seductive from where she sits."

Herb rubs his bald spot thoughtfully. "Ya think?" he asks after a while.

The phone rings while I am patting ground beef into hamburgers for supper. No one has the number so I know it's Herb.

"Consultation," he announces.

"Whenever you get here," I say. "It's just hamburgers."

"Not that," says Herb.

"What?" I ask, unsuspecting.

"Bianca's doctor called me today. She's ovulating."

"Something wrong?" I ask, but without sympathy.

"She's decided to go for it," Herb says. "She wants me for the donor."

"Too bad."

"Wait," says Herb. "I just leave it at his office. The doctor says it would be totally impersonal."

"She's killing me," I say.

"She'd sign a contract. I'd have no obligation, except for this."

"Why are you doing this to me?"

"I have a conflict in the morning," says Herb. "I wanted your permission to skip the doctor's visit and stop at Bianca's after work—just get it over with and come home."

I slam the phone into its cradle. From my greasy hand, it misses and dangles by the cord. Herb's voice rises from the floor, a bit anxious but essentially cheerful, still talking, talking.

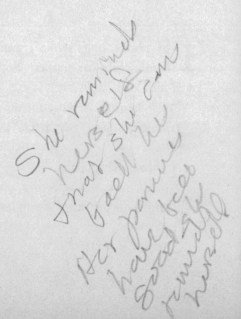